KILTY PLEA

CAROLINE LEE

COPYRIGHT

Copyright © 2023, Caroline Lee
Caroline@CarolineLeeRomance.com

ALL RIGHTS RESERVED. This book contains material protected under International and Federal Copyright Laws and Treaties. Any unauthorized reprint or use of this material is prohibited. No part of this book may be reproduced or transmitted in any form or by any means, electronic or mechanical, including photocopying, recording, or by any information storage and retrieval system without express written permission from the author.

First edition: 2023

Printing/manufacturing information for this book may be found on the last page

Cover: EDHGraphics

ABOUT THIS BOOK

Well, are they married, or aren't they? And does it matter?

When Payton MacIntyre, quiet King's Hunter, is sent to an abbey to challenge the bandits threatening the land, he doesn't expect to ride away with a wife. In fact, he's still not convinced he's actually married to the intriguing Flora, but that's what he tells his family before they can begin their seasonal interrogation about when he'll marry. But what will this new wife of his think when he finally removes his helm and exposes her to his hideously scarred visage?

Desperate to escape the cruel Abbot and find her missing younger brother, Flora goes along with the phony marriage... she just doesn't expect the Hunter to treat her so kindly. He might be reluctant to show his face, but his soft words—and softer touches—leave her breathless. And when he defends her to his family while searching for her brother, Flora falls even more in love.

But Yule is approaching and Flora's growing contentment is threatened by an old danger. Can a fake marriage end in real love for a scarred Hunter, or will her past destroy them both?

Warning: *So* delicious, you'll start your Christmas decadence early! Kick back, enjoy, and get into the holiday spirit with another super-spicy, laugh-out-loud medieval RomCom from Caroline Lee!

PROLOGUE

"To the Hunter! The King's Hunter!"

Payton MacIntyre didn't want to drink, but he had to at least acknowledge the toast. So he stood, lifted his mug, and nodded to the revelers.

They, being halfway to drunk already, gave a mighty cheer at his acknowledgement.

After what they've been through, they'd likely cheer the sound of a bug's fart.

Payton resettled himself in the chair—a finely carved one with a thick cushion—beside the Abbot and rested his untouched mug on his knee.

The Abbot, who was seated in an even finer chair, nodded at the mug. "Ye're no' drinking with us, brother Hunter?"

Payton didn't drink while on assignment, and while this celebration was an indication his assignment was over and he'd soon be on his way to his family's holding for Hogmanay, he still wasn't going to drink with these people.

Or the Abbot.

The whole Abbey of the People itself, really, was creepy as fook, and he wasn't certain why the King *cared* about them.

Still, 'twas easier to fall back on what was expected rather than explain the truth. So, he tapped the steel helmet he always wore on assignment. "This makes it difficult to imbibe, Father."

The Abbot, a man who was only a decade or two older than Payton, with thick brown hair and a winning smile, scoffed good-naturedly. "*Surely* ye must eat and drink while on missions, brother? Ye cannae fault us for offering ye such hospitality after ye've saved us from such evil!"

The man laughed then, his broad gesture encompassing the men and women—and aye, even children—who cavorted and danced below their dais. Payton made a noncommittal noise and lifted the mug in salute, but was careful to place it at the table by his side without drinking.

The helm was constructed such that he *could* lift it just enough to drink or eat if necessary. And of course, he didn't wear it *all* the time…just when he was around others while on a mission.

As his commander had taught him, a Hunter's helmet was a symbol, and symbols were powerful reminders of the King's law and order. The man under the helmet mattered less than the symbol of the King's Hunters in general. It didn't matter *who* maintained the King's laws, as long as they were maintained.

The isolated Abbey of the People in remote, western Campbell land had reported having their lands attacked by bandits. His Majesty, anxious to remain in good standing with the Church, had dispatched Payton, who was on his way to visit his own family.

The bandits had been easy to defeat, especially with the fear the helmet evoked on Payton's side. But he was pleased he didn't have to stay any longer at the Abbey; the short time he spent in the Abbot's company made him wonder if the place was associated with the Church at all.

For one thing, there were no saints venerated, no holy

hours. The people who lived here were a strange mix; there were some monks, aye, but more laymen and their families, and quite a few unmarried lasses as well.

This place was more like a town and less like an abbey... except there *was* a clear and definite leader: their charismatic Abbot, who even now was watching Payton with a sharp gleam in his eyes.

"We are a puir community, brother," he was saying, "and we cannae offer much in thanks other than our food and drink."

Payton made an impatient gesture with his hand. "Nae thanks are necessary, Father. I am doing the King's bidding. Write yer thanks to him."

"Still, we owe ye much, brother."

Fook, always with the 'brother'. Payton got enough of that when he visited his parents' home; here he wasn't a brother any more than these drunken fools were.

His gaze still on the people below, Payton tried not to allow his irritation to creep into his voice. "Ye owe me naught."

"We have much to offer a man such as yerself." The Abbot shifted closer, his breath smelling of something too sweet. "A warrior must celebrate his victories, I ken it. What better way than to sink into the pleasures of the flesh, eh?" When Payton shifted in his chair, torn between intrigue and disgust, the Abbot chuckled almost lewdly. "Food, drink, and a lovely lass."

Payton couldn't help the way his head turned to watch the group of young women who moved among the revelers, their heads down as they offered trays of mugs or bowls of food to others.

One caught his eye; a skinny waif in a too-big gown, her feet bare despite the winter's cold. Lank hair fell into her eyes, and she kept her gaze directed at the ground. But as he watched, one of the men slapped her arse as he passed, and she froze. Slowly, she straightened and sent a glare at the man's back which was fierce enough to make Payton's lips curl beneath his helmet.

She was underfed, aye, but she had a woman's curves and fire in her gaze.

At his side, the Abbot chuckled again. "These women arenae free to be used, brother, although I ken ye have a warrior's urges. There are whores in the next town for those needs; these are *my* lasses, and are meant for marriage."

There was something about the way the Abbot bragged which made Payton's skin crawl. "I understand," he said gruffly, although he didn't. A woman sworn to a holy house should be meant for vows, not marriage.

Either way, ye cannae fook 'em, is the point.

They wouldn't want him, anyway.

"But still, brother..." the Abbot said slyly, "I can see ye have yer eye on one in particular. She shall be yers."

Payton didn't want her—didn't want to spend any more time among these people's company than he had to. But when the Abbot raised his hand to gesture to the wench, he knew he had no choice but to maintain politeness until he could slip away.

Soon he'd be home on MacIntyre land and all this would be behind him.

Soon.

CHAPTER 1

Flora MacGregor did her best to keep from meeting anyone's eyes.

Especially the men's.

And *especially* the Abbot's.

Wincing, she hunched again as she murmured her offer of ale to one of the half-drunk Faithful. The man took it without looking at who was doing the offering, thank the Lord.

Since earning the Abbot's harsh words—and harsher lashes—two days ago after her attempted escape, no one wanted to be seen interacting with her, and that was fine by Flora.

She just had to survive.

Survive, for wee Lenny.

Soon, she often whispered to herself.

But *soon* had turned into months, and now her feet burned from the cold, and the harsh wool of the sackcloth-dress she'd been forced to wear scraped at the scabs forming over the welts on her back.

Soon was starting to feel like *eternity*.

Son of a biscuit!

Mayhap if she could keep her chin down and cease from

riling the Abbot's ire—cease from gaining his attention, in fact—she might survive 'til the spring. Then she could escape and find Lenny, and they'd run as far and as fast from the Abbey of the People as they could.

Soon.

A hand smacked against her rear end and Flora gasped and whirled on the man who'd done it. Thank the good Lord he was too far in his cups to notice her insolence, or she'd likely have to bleed again afore the night was through—to show her repentance.

The man who'd hit her…he hadn't been one of the ones to join the Abbot in *teaching her a lass's place* when she'd first arrived. If he had been, she doubted she would've been able to hold onto her temper long enough to drop her gaze to the ground again.

Where it belonged, according to the Abbot.

Flora blew out a breath.

Easy, lass.

All she had to do was make it through the next few hours. Then she could crawl onto her pallet in the unmarried women's dormitory and try to shut her ears to the sounds of the men "claiming" their rights and pray tonight wouldn't be her night.

The Abbot preached that women should be unsullied when they went to their marriage beds, but apparently when 'twas *his* chosen men doing the sullying, it didn't count.

She frowned and sent a silent prayer to heaven that there was too much ale flowing tonight to have to worry about such things.

"Flora!"

At the sound of *his* voice, Flora's gaze jerked upward, unbidden.

Oh, cheese and crackers, 'twas the Abbot himself gesturing for her to approach.

She glanced away and realized the eyes of many of the Faithful were upon her. There'd be no pretending she didn't hear him. No escape.

Swallowing, she shuffled toward the dais.

"Nay, no' the ale, lass," the Abbot boomed, good-naturedly. "Brother Hunter requires *milk!*"

A mighty cheer went up behind her, and Flora felt her blood rush down into her knees.

Nay nay nay nay nay.

This couldn't be happening.

'Twas *her turn.*

Flora swallowed and forced her knees not to buckle. She swayed, desperately torn between running—where would she go that they could not find her?—and collapsing in the dirt.

'Twas her turn.

Dizzy now, she forced herself to look at the man she would be sold to. This celebration was in his honor, and while she was pleased the bandits were dead, she knew the truth of their actions.

The Hunter is honorable.

Aye, there was that.

They'd all seen that, in the way he faced the bandits, giving them a fair fight.

And she had the impression he didn't exactly approve of the way the Abbot ran things here with the Faithful. So that was another point in his favor.

He is young and braw.

Aye, she reluctantly admitted. But she wasn't certain if that was a point for or against him. In the months she'd been at the Abbey, she'd seen women given in marriage to old men, cruel men. Men who stank of death and disease and greed.

Ye cannae see his face.

Aye, he might not be handsome, but he *was* well-built.

Exceedingly well-built.

"Flora!" the Abbot boomed again, and she knew it mattered not how the Hunter looked, because there was no escape.

'Twas her turn.

Without really seeing, she took the bowl of goat's milk which had been thrust into her hands, and slowly shuffled toward the dais. Oh, how she wished her feet weren't quite so swollen with cold, or her shoulders hunched with pain.

Her father had always said pride would be her downfall, but now 'twas all she had to wrap around herself to stay warm.

Flora focused her gaze on the milk in the bowl, trying to keep her hands from shaking, trying to keep the surface of the liquid ripple-free.

It didn't quite work.

The wood of the dais was slightly warmer beneath her feet, but only enough to send pinpricks of pain across her skin. Swallowing, she knelt before the Hunter, her attention on the man's knees as the Abbot's voice praised her.

They were quite nice knees.

"...Meek and mild, Brother Hunter, and I think ye'll find her to yer taste. I've gone through much effort to ensure she is as pure as when she came to us, and ye can imagine, 'twas difficult."

Strong knees. He wore naught between his kilt and his boots, and Flora couldn't help but wonder if he was as cold as she. If so, he showed no signs of it—nor of appreciating the Abbot's ribald joke at her expense.

Her cheeks were heating, and for once, she appreciated the embarrassment, because it might keep her warm.

His kilt was the King's colors, which was traditional, and the bit between the woolen material and his knees was... *His thighs, ye ninny. They're his thighs. Everyone has them.*

Nay, not everyone had thighs like these.

Suddenly, the idea of being sold to this man didn't seem so terrible.

At least there wouldn't be an old man slavering atop her as she clenched her eyes shut and tried not to breathe. *Her duty*, the Abbot and the other lasses had called it...but Flora had a different duty.

To her younger brother.

Her heart began to thump in her chest at the thought of Lenny.

If she was to be given to this man, she wouldn't be able to find her little brother, would she?

All thoughts of the man's knees fled from her mind and instinctively she lifted her gaze to his.

Or to where his would be, were his eyes not hidden by the deep shadows of the helmet. It made him look fierce, terrifying, especially with her on her knees before him.

If ye are given to him, ye cannae save Lenny.

She began to shake.

The man moved faster than he had a right to.

One moment, he was sitting upright, his hands—which had wielded his sword with such deadly accuracy only hours before—curled around the arms of his chair.

The next, he was leaning toward her, one hand reaching for her...

She wanted to lean away, to protest... But her breaths were coming too fast and she was frozen in place.

His hand closed around her shoulder, big and warm and...comforting?

"Flora," he murmured.

Or at least, she *thought* that might've been what he'd said, but the helmet's echo was such that he could've muttered something about *oral* or *the Torah* or her *aura*.

Fish sticks, he was a man; 'twas more likely he spoke of *oral*, aye?

But...at his touch, her breathing had calmed, her heart had

slowed. She stared up into the two dark holes where his eyes should be, and she wondered what he saw.

"Flora has a drink for ye, brother Hunter." The Abbot murmured slyly as he leaned closer. "Go on, lass. Honor the warrior the only way ye have."

She had no choice.

Something like a leaden weight had settled in her stomach, and she lifted the bowl of milk to the man who now loomed over her. "Drink of the milk, brother," she intoned dully, repeating the words she'd heard almost a dozen times since her arrival at the Abbey.

'Twas either this or feel the Abbot's lash again.

The pull of the welts on her back forced her to tighten her jaw and keep her arms steady.

Take the milk, she prayed, silently urging him. The Hunter had taken no food or drink from the Faithful this evening; she'd been watching.

If he turned her down now, she'd likely not live through the night.

When his hand moved from her shoulder to close around the bowl, she breathed a sigh of relief.

He used his other hand to lift his helmet just far enough that she could see a strong jaw, lined with dark stubble, as he brought the bowl to his mouth and drank from it.

She slumped.

'Twas done. She belonged to the Hunter.

What of Lenny?

Mayhap life with the Hunter would make it easier to escape and look for her brother. Aye, she'd willingly put up with his pawing and manly urges, no matter how painful, if it meant she was away from the Abbey and closer to finding Lenny.

He was her responsibility, and she'd failed him once already.

When the Hunter lowered the bowl, 'twas mostly empty,

but Flora knew what the Abbot expected. Lifting it to her lips, she finished what remained, and tried to savor the thick, delicious broth.

"Good!" boomed the Abbot, and behind her, the Faithful cheered.

Enough ale has flowed this night that they would cheer a badger, were one to wander by.

The Abbot had continued the ceremonial words—fellowship, debts being paid, blah blah blah. But Flora found her gaze held by the dark shadows of the Hunter's helmet.

What did he see when he looked down at her?

When the Abbot finished his speech, his followers cheered, and he rose to his feet—unsteadily, Flora noticed—to move among them. Leaving her kneeling on the dais at the Hunter's feet.

Ye belong to him now. Ye're safe from the Abbot.

But, plucking heck, would she be safe from *the Hunter*?

"Flora," he said again, taking the empty bowl from her hand and moving it to the table at his side. "Ye must be cold."

And that's when he took both of her hands in his and pulled her to her feet. 'Twas such an effortless movement, she gasped, both in surprise and in fright. How could his touch be so warm, when the air was so frigid, this close to the dead of winter?

"Lass?" he prompted, and he had a lovely voice, didn't he? Low and gravely, as if it wasn't often used.

What had he asked? Flora forced her gaze to his chest, so she could think. "Aye, S-Sir Hunter," she managed. "'Tis chilly."

It took a moment to realize the noise he made was supposed to be *laughter*. "'Tis a bit more than chilly, I would think. Here."

With that, he stood, and she gasped again, because he was so very much larger than her. Flora stepped back so they wouldn't be crowded, but in doing so her numb foot slipped from the dais. She teetered—

And one of his large arms wrapped around her waist, pulling her forward. Saving her.

Behind her, another cheer went up, but Flora couldn't process it. All she knew was that she was *warm*. The Hunter's helm made him seem cold and distant, but his body…

Saints protect us, his body was so warm, she wanted to press herself against him and never back away.

Mayhap 'twas why the Faithful were cheering, because of her reaction to this man.

Focus, Flora.

Aye. Aye, she might be his now, but he was naught more than a means to an end. An escape.

So she forced herself to plant her palms against his chest—so warm, so warm!—and push away. "Thank ye, Sir Hunter," she whispered, her gaze on the heavy brooch which held his cloak closed at the neck.

"Ye dinnae call me 'brother'?"

Was that amusement in his tone?

Please, God, let him be good-natured. Let him help me.

She considered her words without lifting her gaze. "Ye are no' my brother," she said in a low voice, hoping the Abbot couldn't hear the risk she was taking. "And the Abbot is no' my father."

"Ah, a dissenter in the ranks." He made that noise again, the raspy sort of chuckle. Then his hands rose to the brooch at which she'd been staring, and he unclasped it. "Here."

Before she could understand his intentions, the man had swung his fur-lined cloak from his shoulders and settled it around hers.

The thing weighed as much as she did, and Flora's protesting knees threatened to give under the burden. But…

But it still carried his heat.

It smelled of him, and 'twas *warm*. Warmer than she'd been since she'd come to this place of constant fear and chill and worry.

His large hands settled beneath her chin, so she had to tip her head back to stare up at him. It took a moment to realize he was re-fastening the brooch.

He was *giving* her the cloak?

"Oh," she breathed.

"There." His hands settled on her shoulders. "Now ye'll no' be cold, lass."

"Flora," she corrected in a whisper, then shook her head, determined not to be wooed by the first hint of kindness in months. "Will ye no' be cold, Sir Hunter?"

One of his shoulders hitched, a little shrug. "'Tis no' so far to MacIntyre land. I'll no' freeze between here and there."

Her breath had frozen. *MacIntyre Land.*

'Tis where Lenny was.

Praying her heart wouldn't pound from her chest, she forced a deep breath and tried for nonchalance when she said, "Ye're headed to MacIntyre land, then?"

"Aye, lass. *Flora*. I'm headed home for the Hogmanay celebrations—'tis why the King had me stop here to handle yer wee problem."

Six bandits were a *wee problem*?

Flora was shaking again, but this time not in cold. "Ye're a MacIntyre, then?" she whispered.

"Payton MacIntyre, at yer service." He stepped back and gave a respectful nod. "I'm the laird's third son, and the whole family can be overwhelming at times, if ye ken my meaning."

Nay. Nay, she didn't. It had only ever been her father, Lenny, and herself, alone in the crofter's hut.

But...*shut the front door*! He was a MacIntyre! He was going to the MacIntyre holding.

Thank the good Lord, her prayers were finally answered!

"Ye—ye're leaving soon?" 'Twouldnae do to sound too eager, but 'twas hard to contain her excitement.

He cocked his head to one side, and for the first time she realized she *missed* the way his hands had rested upon her shoulders. Not just their warmth or comforting size, but...

She'd felt safe for the first time in a long while.

"'Tis too late to leave now the sun has set, lass. I'll leave early in the morning and will be home in a few days."

"I..." She was leaving this place. She was leaving! "I cannae wait," she said simply.

"For me to be gone?" There was amusement in his voice.

"To say good riddance to the Abbey."

Suddenly, it felt as if her chest were lighter than possible. Her smile burst free, nearly shocking her with its intensity.

Behind the helmet, she heard him suck in a breath, but she couldn't stop to wonder why. Impulsively, she reached for the man's hand once more, taking it in both of hers.

"Ye'll no' regret this, Payton, I swear it."

Another smile, and then she turned, his cloak still heavy—and warm—about her shoulders and hurried toward the Abbey. Tonight, she wouldn't sleep with the other unmarried women in the dormitory; she didn't trust the Abbot's promises.

Nay, now she had this cloak, she'd spend the night waiting for Payton.

Waiting for her husband.

CHAPTER 2

THE AIR WAS crisp and colder than Payton had expected, in the dim pre-dawn light.

What do ye expect? Ye gave away yer nice warm cloak.

Aye, and he might suffer a bit for it, but 'twas for a good cause.

The woman—the waif...*Flora.* Flora had needed it more than he, and Payton knew a little discomfort would be worth it, knowing she'd be warm.

Damnation, she'd not even worn stockings, had she? At first, as he'd watched her, he'd thought her some sort of slave... except the Scots kept no slaves, not anymore. Then he'd decided she was being punished for some reason, made to suffer in the cold.

But when the Abbot had called her over...

Christ, he was still ashamed of how his body had reacted to having her kneeling at his feet.

She'd been so close to him—to his knees, his thighs, his cock—and he'd had to struggle to control his arousal.

She was too dirty and too skinny and too miserable for ye to lust after.

Aye, he was glad he'd given neither her nor the Abbot an indication of his inappropriate interest.

But...she'd offered him milk.

He didn't want to share the Abbot's ale, but when she'd made him such a simple offering, Payton didn't see the harm in it. They shared the milk, he'd caught her in his arms when she might've fallen, they spoke of his family. And she'd smiled.

Oh, Christ, she'd smiled.

Even this morning, the memory of that smile—the way it had transformed her face from something waifish into an ethereal beauty—still made him shift uncomfortably in the saddle.

In that moment, he hadn't wanted her because he'd been too long without a woman and she was kneeling submissively at his feet. He'd wanted her because she was lovely.

Not lovely in a traditional sense, or the *lovely* of the ladies at court; the angles of her face were too harsh, her teeth too crooked, the lines around her eyes too distinct to be *that* kind of lovely. Nay, she was the *lovely* of strength, and certainty, and joy.

Lovely, and joyous, and sparkling—everything a woman should be.

And he was a scarred monster hiding under a helm.

I cannae wait to say good riddance to the Abbey.

That's what she'd said, and he still wasn't certain what she'd meant, but he'd agreed with her. Which is why he was up at the arse-crack of dawn and riding out before any of the hungover abbey denizens were up and about.

Good riddance.

His horse snorted and tossed her head, breath fogging in the cold air, and Payton shook his head, dragging himself back to the here and now.

The Abbot and his people might've been creepy as fook, but they're behind ye now.

He'd done his duty to his King; now he had to look to the future.

The immediate future.

The oh-fook-two-days-from-now-he'd-be-home future.

Da would give him shite about when he was going to finally get his head out of his arse and take over the management of the tower house by the loch from Daniel.

Daniel would nag him about his devotion to the Church and how 'twas only Payton's egotism keeping him—Daniel—from focusing on his flock as necessary.

The girls wouldn't let him rest until Payton had sketched—actually fooking *sketched*—the latest fashions from court.

Rupert would make snide remarks about Payton's freedom to go "gallivanting about, saving the world" while his wife showed off her latest fat bairn.

And Mam…Mam would give him hell about finding a nice wife and settling down like his brother Rupert had done.

Shite. Was it no wonder he returned home increasingly rarely these days?

Sighing, Payton reached up to scrub a hand across his face and bumped against the helm. He'd forgotten he was wearing it—it had become second nature, on this mission in particular.

Most of the King's Hunters removed the helmet once they defeated the bad guys, or once they no longer had to intimidate. For Payton, 'twas easier to wear the damned thing than to have to field questions about his scar.

And at the Abbey… Well, he might have defeated the bandits, but he'd never felt comfortable enough to show his real face, so he'd kept it on. And last night he'd slept in it, sitting up in the stables, ready to head out at first light.

The horse tossed its head again, and Payton frowned in the shadows. Why was the animal so unsettled?

He sniffed the air but was unable to smell aught besides *himself* inside the steel cage. Pushing himself up in the stirrups, he ignored the bite of the wind around his thighs as he strained his senses in all directions.

The horse continued to pick her way along the road, and Payton had just decided to remove the helm so he could see what was necessary...when a bundle came into view.

'Twas a smallish bundle, thrown haphazardly on the side of the road next to a ditch. The sort of bundle which might've been refuse...or might've been a once-fine fur-lined cloak, wrapped around a small frame.

He was on the ground before he'd realized he'd left his saddle.

Kneeling beside the bundle, Payton realized he was holding his breath, and not just because of the cold air. Nay, he was terrified of what he might find when he rolled the bundle over.

Best to get it done, lad.

His hand didn't shake as he reached out for the fur, but only by dint of will.

When he uncovered her face—still, pale, perfectly imperfect—he felt his heart clench in his chest. Sorrow. Anger. Guilt.

But then...

But then Flora's little nose scrunched and her lips turned into a frown, and his breath *whooshed* out of him in one big burst, creating enough steam to fog his vision of her. When it cleared, she was blinking woozily up at him, and her lips had curled into a smile.

"Good morning," she managed, before a yawn interrupted her.

Damn her, how could she be so cheerful when he'd just had the scare of his life? His voice might've reflected this anger when he pulled her upright.

"What are ye doing here?"

"Waiting for ye." Yawning again, she stretched and looked around. "I was hoping I'd chosen the correct road, but I wanted to get as far away from the Abbey as possible." She pushed away his hand and sat cross-legged as she pulled her lanky hair over one shoulder. "I'm pleased I caught ye."

"I'm no'," he grumbled, sitting back on his haunches, although 'twas a lie. "Why would ye sleep out here all night, lass? And risk freezing?"

"Och, I wasnae freezing," she corrected him, clearly one of those cheerful morning people. Her fingers flew as she plaited her braid. "'Tis been many months since I was this warm, thanks to yer fur." Suddenly, she ducked her chin, as if embarrassed. "And I told ye why I'm here—to wait for ye."

"But *why*?"

"Because I wasnae certain where ye were sleeping last night, so this was the only way I kenned to catch ye in time."

An inkling was coming to Payton. "Ye...cannae mean to come with me?"

Flora's head snapped up, and he realized her eyes were a lovely shade of greenish-brown, not the blue he'd guessed last night. And now they were full of panic.

"Of course I mean to come with ye!" she declared, tossing her braid over her shoulder and scrambling to her knees. "Ye cannae leave me!"

"Why no'?" he shrugged. "The Abbey is yer home, aye? The Abbot will likely worry when he wakes and finds ye missing."

Now she was kneeling, the panic in her gaze creeping toward desperation. "Nay, he'll expect it! If ye *do* send me back, I'll no' go!"

Payton shook his head, admitting he was lost, but trying to hold his temper. "'Twill cost me a few hours, but I can make them up tomorrow. I can turn around and escort ye back."

"Nay!" Flora lunged for him, latching on to his forearm, and Payton was surprised by the warmth which shot up his arm. "Nay, please," she finished in a whisper. "If ye do, he'll kill me."

He stared, dumbfounded. *What?*

Perhaps his expression asked the question because she swallowed and tightened her hold slightly.

"Please, Sir Hunter. Two months back, one of the lasses was returned by the man she was given to. I dinnae ken the reason, only that she was verra afraid of him. The Abbot…he called her sullied, and nae good to him." Flora was shaking now. "She disappeared the next night, and the other women—they whispered he'd killed her himself."

"Fook," muttered Payton under his breath. He didn't understand this, but he did understand her fear. "Come here."

'Twas awkward to pull her against him while he crouched, so he stood as he tugged, and ended with her tucked up under his chin, his arms around her back, holding her close. She was warm, aye, but still she shivered.

In fear.

He hated it.

They stood in silence, with him rubbing her back, for a long minute. Finally, he murmured, "Why would the Abbot kill yer friend?"

"She wasnae my friend. I had nae friends there—none of us did. 'Twasnae allowed."

That didn't make sense. Why did she choose to live in such a strange, remote place, if she wasn't allowed friends? 'Twas clear Flora had no love for the Abbey of the People, or the founder.

He tried asking in another way. "Why would he kill her?"

Beneath his chin, she made a little snorting noise. "I told ye." Her voice was muffled by the fur and by his chest, but he could still understand. "She wasnae any use to him. That's why we were there—to be useful to him. To be given away. Once we're sullied, we cannae be gifted to his friends or used to pay debts."

Payton's hand had stilled against her back, and now his fingers spread, as if he could keep her from harm. A terrible suspicion had lodged in his brain and now crept forward. "The Abbot...he *gave* ye away? As what?"

A *slave*?

She bumped his chin when she tipped her head back to stare up into his eyes. "He didnae explain? The ceremony?"

Oh fook.

Payton's heart was thundering in his chest. "What ceremony?"

The milk—the words...he had a terrible suspicion he wasn't going to like what she said next.

"The Abbot gave me to ye, Sir Hunter," she whispered, her hazel eyes skipping across the imposing features of his helmet. "I'm yer wife."

Nay.

Nay.

The word had to be said or his head would likely explode. "*Nay.*"

She exhaled, a wry little twist of her lips. "I ken 'tis no' what ye're used to—"

"What *I'm* used to?" He was shaking his head as he planted his hands on Flora's shoulders and pushed her away far enough that he could lower his chin and glare at her. "Look, lass—"

"Flora," she corrected unhelpfully.

"Look, *Flora*, I dinnae ken what kind of bullshite the Abbot fed ye, but we're *no'* married. A bowl of milk is *no'* a wedding ceremony."

"Och, I ken that," she said dismissively, flapping a hand about. "But the Abbot believes—actually..." She frowned and tapped her lower lip as she stared at where his left ear used to be. "Actually, I doubt he even actually believes it. But his *followers* do, and that's how he stays in power."

"By *gifting* wives to me? As if ye're a loaf of bread?" Payton's voice rose in his disbelief. "Or a horse?"

Flora snorted and pulled the cloak tighter around herself.

"Dingleberries, the Abbot would likely prefer a horse. No' as willful as I am," she muttered.

Christ. What was he supposed to do now?

She belonged at the Abbey...didn't she?

Payton realized his fingers were digging into her shoulders, as if he didn't want to let her go.

"And..." His voice was hoarse. "If ye return?"

"I told ye." She sniffed once, her gaze back on his ear. Or mayhap the tree behind him. Or naught at all. "I'll be of nae use, because all of his followers will see me as sullied."

Fook fook fook.

"So, I *have* to take ye with me?"

Was it his imagination, or was there a flash of hurt in her eyes before she ducked her chin? "If ye dinnae want a wife—"

"I dinnae *have* a wife, Flora!" he burst out. "I have an unwanted, half-frozen *reward* thrust upon me, with a side helping of guilt, and ye dinnae—" He shifted her out of the way long enough to glance at her feet. "Aye, ye *still* dinnae even have *shoes!*"

Her shoulders hunched, and she sniffed again. "He took them from me when I was brought to the Abbey," she said in a small voice. "Because I had to learn obedience."

Payton struggled to control his breathing. "Aye? And when was that?"

"In the early spring. Afore the thaw."

Nine months or more? *Jesu Christo*, 'twas a miracle she hadn't lost her toes. Payton blew out a breath. "So...ye couldnae even *fake* obedience?"

Mayhap 'twas the hint of teasing in his voice which convinced her to peek up at him. "I can fake many things, Sir Hunter."

Beneath the helm, his nose wrinkled in disapproval. He hated the thought of what else she'd *faked*. What she'd *had* to fake.

That smile?

What in St. Bart's name was going on here? Two days ago, all he had to dread was the thought of his family's ambush when he returned home, and how to avoid them until he could return to the King's side.

Now? Now he had a wife—

Nay ye dinnae.

Right. He had to remember that. They both drank some milk; there was naught about *that* in the Church's wedding ceremony!

"I'm sorry," she whispered, so low he might've missed it.

"What?" His fingers tightened on her shoulders again, causing her to wince and him to sigh. "Sorry."

"Nay, I'm sorry." Flora lifted her gaze to his, which was remarkable, knowing she couldn't actually *see* his eyes. "I'm sorry ye're stuck with me. *Fragglerock*, I didnae want it either—"

"Because I'm..." He trailed off, realizing she couldn't see his scar, didn't know how flawed he was. "Because I'm a Hunter?" he finished.

But her mouth had dropped open. "Ye are brave and honorable and strong, and ye seem a good man. Any of the women in the unmarried dormitory would be *grateful* to have been given to ye. But I..." She shook her head slightly. "I didnae want to be given. Until I realized where..."

Payton blew out a breath. This wasn't making any sense. "Where what?"

She was studying him. As he watched, she drew her lower lip between her teeth, worrying it as if she was considering what to say to him.

And that sight?

That sight went *right* to his cock. Reached around it and stroked.

If he closed his eyes right now, he could picture what she'd look like on her knees again, his cock between those lips, those big hazel eyes staring up at him. He tightened his hold on her to keep from reaching beneath his kilt and touching himself like a degenerate.

Flora's eyes had darkened to almost a gray-blue as she studied him, and now she released her lower lip with a *pop*.

He didn't groan, but 'twas close.

"I need to get away from the Abbey, Sir Hunter," she whispered, almost pleading. "Please understand."

"Och, I understand, lass." He wanted away, too. "I'll—I'll take ye."

As suddenly as that, Flora collapsed. 'Twas as if her knees gave out, and she would've sunk to the ground, had he not caught her and pulled her against him once more.

And a very real part of him was screaming *That's where she belongs!*

While the logical part of his brain reminded him he'd only set eyes on her the night before.

What the hell was going on that he was reacting so viscerally, so *primally*, to a woman he'd only just met?

"I'll take ye, lass," he murmured again. But to remind himself this *wasn't* a permanent solution, he continued, "As far as the next village. Ye'll be safe from the Abbot there."

He hoped.

Flora had stiffened against him when he'd added his caveat, but she didn't pull away, didn't argue.

Thank Christ.

He was one of the King's Hunters. He didn't have time for a wife, even if she needed *him*.

The battle with the bandits was behind him, but the bigger war was coming: His family.

Payton needed all his wits about him to survive *that* war unscathed and return to the King's side where he belonged. He didn't need to be worrying about a dirty, too-thin bundle of rags who'd smiled at him as if he offered salvation.

"Please, Payton," she whispered.

And deep within the shadows of his helmet, his eyes closed on a shudder.

She remembered his name?

Why did she look at him as if he was her hero?

Why did he want to *be* her hero?

"Just the next village," he choked out, reminding himself as much as her.

And he pretended not to hear the little sound she made which might've been another sniff.

He had to focus on the next mission in order to survive it. But he could take her as far as civilization and leave her there, knowing she'd be safe.

"How far will that be?" she finally asked.

How far? "Tomorrow evening," he guessed, remembering how remote this part of Campbell land was—'twas likely why the Abbot had chosen this location. "Tonight we'll camp, and tomorrow there'll be a real inn."

And the day after that…MacIntyre Keep.

In his arms, Flora took a shuddering, deep breath, and straightened. "Good." She nodded once then pulled away from him. "Good," she repeated, not sounding like herself. "Then I have two days to convince ye no' to leave me."

Saying that, she nodded again and marched toward the horse.

It would've been more impressive had she not stepped hard atop a stick and hissed, then had to hobble the rest of the way.

Shaking his head, Payton followed.

Two days. He could do this.

Only two days.

Then he'd be free of Flora.

Why did he hate that thought?

CHAPTER 3

This wasn't the first time Flora had known the next few hours could be the difference between life and death for her. Sugar sticks, when the bandits had killed her father and burned their croft, she'd been desperate to save Lenny. When they'd deposited her at the Abbey on the Abbot's orders, she'd used every sense God had given her to figure out how to stay alive and be useful.

And now?

Well, now Payton MacIntyre was the only one who could take her to her brother.

Dang it all to heck.

She just had to prove she wouldn't be a burden.

Surely, they were only a matter of days from MacIntyre land? Once there, *someone* would be able to tell her of a lad with flaxen hair and two different colored eyes? *Surely* someone would remember Lenny?

All she had to do was convince Payton to take her that far instead of the next village.

God willing.

Sighing, Flora bit her lip to stay awake, determined to think of a way to prove her usefulness to the Hunter.

"Go to sleep, lass."

She started, bumping the back of her head against his helm and earning a sigh from him. They were the first words he'd said to her since early that morning when he'd pulled her into his lap atop his horse and wrapped one arm around her to hold the reins.

Twisting, she tried to peer up at him, but the angle was all wrong.

"What?"

"I can tell ye're fighting sleep, Flora. Close yer eyes. I'll no' let ye fall."

She could just see his jaw—with the dark stubble a little thicker today—move when he spoke, and she told herself that shouldn't be as fascinating as 'twas.

"*Fudge,*" she murmured, still watching that bit of skin. "I'm no' tired."

He snorted, the sound echoing strangely in the helmet. "I cannae imagine ye slept well on the hard ground—"

"'Twas nae harder than the stones I slept on in the dormitory," she hurried to assure him, "and yer cloak kept me warmer than I've been in a long while."

He didn't speak for a while after that, but she felt the muscles in his arm tense.

She was sitting on his lap, her arse resting atop the thick cloak, which did little to cushion her from his hard thighs, but she didn't mind.

Finally, he exhaled. "The Abbey really is a shite place, is it no'?"

She didn't want to speak about the Abbey. "I'm with ye now. Ye're taking me away from there." Did she sound too eager? Love a duck. "I can be useful, Sir Hunter."

"Call me Payton," he growled.

Payton.

She shifted in place and was surprised when his free hand clamped down atop her knee, holding her in place.

"Stop that."

Stop moving?

Oh.

She was suddenly, *acutely*, painfully and wonderfully aware that his thighs weren't the *only* thing hard beneath her buttocks. Something long and hard pressed against the cleft of her arse, and her eyes widened when she realized what 'twas.

Payton MacIntyre, the honorable King's Hunter who'd said he wanted no wife…was aroused.

By *her*.

Well, *suck a duck*.

Completely unbidden, Flora's hand rose to her braid and she tugged at the tip. Even when she'd lived under her father's roof and been allowed to eat her fill and heat her own water for her bath, she'd never been considered beautiful.

Her eyes were too wideset, her teeth too crooked, her build too skinny—too much like a lad's, Da had always said—to attract a man.

Of course, her months at the Abbey had taught her that men might *claim* they wanted a beautiful woman, but they could be satisfied with a lass who would stay quiet as they pawed and groped her, no matter how she looked.

But Payton…

She'd thought him different.

Clearly, he wasn't.

She hadn't bathed in months, she was half-starved, and she was fairly certain something small and multi-legged had taken up residence in her chemise. But he was still aroused, just by holding her?

He's a King's Hunter. He's no' that desperate for female companionship.

Except…evidence said he was.

Ye can use this.

"I can be useful," she murmured again, before she'd even thought the words through.

Aye.

If the Hunter wanted her, and he could get her to her brother…

Well, she wouldn't be the first woman to trade her body to achieve her goal, would she? And thanks to the Abbot, their mating would be at least sanctioned.

And ye cannae lie to yerself. Ye wouldnae mind him *being the one to paw over yer body.*

This was true.

"Come here," he muttered under his breath, which confused her, until his arm closed around her middle and he pulled her off-balance, causing her to yelp and grab for him.

"Cheese and rice!"

Chuckling, he murmured something she couldn't quite make out, and continued to move her.

She'd been half-expecting him to toss her to the ground, but instead, he pulled one of her legs over the saddle, until she was… Well, there was no other word for it; she was sitting in his lap.

His arm was still at her back, holding the reins, but he paid no attention to the road ahead. Instead, he reached for one of her feet, and pulled it toward him.

This meant she had to either willingly toss herself from his lap, or lean heavily into his chest, while risking knee dislocation.

"Ow!"

Obviously, she chose the knee dislocation.

"Shush." She could hear the smile in his voice, which was… strange. Nice? "Ye've seriously been without shoes for almost a year?"

Flora would've answered, except at that moment, he pressed the pad of his thumb into the arch of her foot, and the sensation—

—pain—

—relief—

—fear—

—Was so great that she gasped, tears coming to her eyes.

"Och, well, I suppose 'tis a good thing ye can still feel pain there. Ye're no' in immediate danger of losing a foot to the cold."

Pain?

Pain?

Now his thumb was rubbing her foot, his large fingers cradling the top, and Flora had to turn her head away to hide the tears in her eyes.

Poop on a stick.

He was…caring for her.

She bit down on her lower lip, hard.

The sensation his fingers caused was torture—pain radiated as the blood began to flow back into the limb, aye. But worse was the way he murmured soothingly under his breath, as if she were a skittish horse or a frightened child, making her chest tighten.

"There," he finally said, as he lowered her foot gently and reached for his saddlebags. "If I pass ye a length of cloth, could ye tear it in half and wrap yer feet?"

"A-aye," she managed, reaching for the undyed wool he offered. She cleared her throat while she busied herself with the project. "'Twas what I was using for most of the winter, ye ken. One of the men pitied me and offered me some cloth to wrap my calves and feet—son of a biscuit, 'twas much better."

Something rumbled in Payton's chest. "I see why ye were so desperate to be away from that place, lass."

Flora didn't bother answering, but kept her attention on her task. Her eyes had filled with tears, and she blinked furiously, praying he wouldn't see them.

"Dinnae fash," he said quietly. "I have ye now."

A single tear fell onto her lap as she leaned forward, and 'twas all she could do to keep from falling apart at his soft vow.

Tears of yearning, aye, but also anger. *She* wanted to be the useful one.

The way things were going, with his touches and caring heart, she'd be half in love with him by the time they reached the next village, and that wouldn't do. 'Twas her mission to make *him* need *her*, even if that meant making use of her body the way the Abbot had intended her to do.

Which is why, hours later when they finally stopped for the night, she had a plan in place.

If they'd be in the next village by tomorrow evening, then this was her only chance to convince him to take her farther.

They made camp in a hollow beside what *would* have been a picturesque stream, were it the height of summer. Since 'twas only a fortnight from Hogmanay, whatever water had once flowed was now frozen over, with snow piled atop.

Flora was exhausted, despite having done naught more tiring than sat atop the Hunter's lap all day. The poor horse was the one who'd had to pick its way through snowbanks, or along narrow trails in the snow which were once roads. Even Payton seemed ready for sleep.

Instead, however, he spent some time building a fire—protected on two sides by the deep walls of the hollow—and preparing a simple dinner of leftover meat from last night's feast, and bannock cakes.

Despite the dry blandness of the oatcakes, Flora ate as if she was ravenous—she was!—and offered to set up the water skin to melt snow over the fire.

Be useful, by golly!

Unfortunately, Payton seemed lost in his thoughts, and

didn't seem to notice her helpful offers, or her attempts at a welcoming smile.

Ye likely have spinach stuck in yer teeth.

'Twas possible, but since it had been several months since she'd last had the leafy green vegetable, she hoped not. More likely Payton was just preoccupied.

Well, 'twas her responsibility to *un*-occupy him. Or rather, occupy him with something else entirely.

Her opportunity came when he finished packing up the leftover food and hung the bundle in a nearby tree to keep it safe from scavengers. Then he left their little camp to find more firewood. Aye, he'd return to find her *helpful*, alright.

When Payton was out of sight, Flora scrambled to her feet and lunged for his saddle and things. She removed the bedroll she'd seen tied there and spent some time laying it out just right; tucking it between the rocks and the fire, so 'twould be as warm and comfortable as possible.

Then she removed the cloak he'd lent her, which she'd been wearing all day despite her offer to return it. Smoothing it out atop the bedroll, she then stepped back to admire her handwork.

'Twas no love nest, but 'twould do.

Flora took the time to scrub her hands and face with snow. A proper seduction should include a scented bath and fine fabrics…but since they were stuck out here in craptastic snow, she'd have to make do.

Judging from the thick staff pressing against her arse cheek all day, Sir Hunter wasn't above pawing at a dirty lass when the need arose. She'd have to count on it.

When she heard him returning, Flora hurried to unlace her bulky borrowed gown, tugging open the brown wool so it gaped at the front, exposing her chemise. She tugged down the stained linen to expose her breasts, gasping as the cold caused her nipples to pebble.

Payton stepped into the circle of firelight, got a good look at her, and dropped the stack of firewood he'd collected onto his foot.

Hopefully 'twas a good sign?

"Fook, lass!" he snarled, hopping about on the other foot, his eyes still glued to her chest. "What in the everloving fook are ye doing?"

Let's see…how would a temptress respond? Flora placed her index finger against her jaw, then dragged it down her throat in what she hoped was a sensual motion, and not the sign of someone choking on a chicken bone.

"Why, Payton," she murmured, aspiring for a sensual tone, "I'm seducing ye."

"Are ye well? Did ye catch a cold?" He stepped over the pile of wood, reaching for her. "Yer voice sounds all scratchy and broken."

"*Son of a beaver*, Payton, I'm trying to be sensual!"

The man had her by the shoulders now, and to her consternation, was looking at her *eyes*, instead of her tits.

"Why?" he asked, seeming genuinely confused.

Flora resisted the urge to roll her eyes. "Because I'm trying to *arouse* ye," *Ye stupid man*, she added in the privacy of her own head. "To prove ye need me."

"I…" He shook his head but didn't release her. "Flora, I dinnae *need* ye."

"Mayhap…" She lowered her voice. "But ye want me."

Without thinking, and before he could respond, she reached out and brushed her palm over the place where his plaid had tented. As her fingers closed around his erect cock, he hissed and stepped back.

Leaving her no choice but to fall to her knees in front of him.

He darn well didn't step any farther back, did he?

"Flora…" His voice was choked, but he said naught more,

and not for the first time, she desperately wished she could see his expression.

"Please, Payton." She lifted her hands toward the lump in his kilt, but at the last second—remembering the shock which had flown up her arm at the last touch—settled for placing them on the outside of his thighs. "Please take me with ye to yer home."

"What?"

As she dragged her hands up the sides of his thighs, his helmeted head dropped back with a groan so she could see his strong throat and jaw by the light of the fire.

"St. Bart's left testicle, lass…"

This seemed encouraging.

Flora shuffled closer on her knees, until her mouth was only inches from—from *him*. She could lift his kilt and gather his member in her hands. She could *taste* him.

If she wanted.

Och, ye want to, dinnae lie.

Well…she *did*. But just because she was trying to seduce him into taking her to MacIntyre land, right? No other reason.

Definitely not a reason having to do with the liquid heat radiating from her core. She pressed her thighs together, swallowed down a whimper at the intense sensation, and peered up at Payton.

"If ye promise to take me to yer home, to MacIntyre land *with ye*…I'll do whatever ye want me to do. Without complaining."

There. 'Twas a suitably arousing seduction, aye? An invitation like that, no man could refuse, great googly-moogly!

But Payton just groaned again, lifting one hand to his face—or where his face would be, were it not covered by a steel helmet.

"Payton?"

"Nay, lass."

Nay?

Flora bit her lip. "Why no'?"

The blasted man actually took a step back, leaving her holding naught but air. "Because ye dinnae want this."

This was *not* how a seduction was supposed to go, for certes. Shame was beginning to creep over Flora and she felt her cheeks heating—a strange sensation in contrast to the cold against her chest.

"I-I do," she insisted, even as she tugged her chemise up to cover her breasts.

"Ye dinnae want to touch *me*." Payton blew out a breath, then bent down to take her shoulders and gently lift her to her feet. "Ye're just using me."

"Aye," she admitted, distracted as he began to lace up her bodice. "But-but ye could use me in return."

He said naught, his head bent low as his fingers flew up her gown, tucking her in and ensuring she was nice and warm. Finally, his fingers rested at the top of the bodice, the base of her throat.

Without looking up—mayhap he was staring at his fingers—he said in a deceptively low voice, "Is that the sort of man ye think me to be, Flora?"

Only a fool would miss the anger in his tone, and in that moment, she wasn't certain what to think anymore.

"*Ye* married me!" The wail burst from her lips before she could stop it. "Why would I no' think that?"

She was shaking now, aye, and mayhap 'twas because of the cold. But the fear was back, and the anger too. At least with the seduction plan, she'd *had* a plan, a chance to be in control.

Now?

With him holding her so gently, but with anger in his tone?

Flamingo feathers, she wished she could see his expression!

"I didnae ken that," he reminded her, his hands moving to her shoulders. "Remember, Flora? That was yer Abbot's idea, no' mine. I agreed to take ye to the next village—."

"Please—." Her voice broke on a sob. *"Please."*

Only, she wasn't certain what she was begging for.

Please dinnae leave me.

Mayhap he heard the unspoken words, because with a muttered, "Fooking hell," he shook his head and pulled her into his arms.

'Twas becoming a familiar place to be held, tucked up under his metal chin, and Flora felt…

Warm.

Protected.

Safe.

One hand stroked her back as she sobbed against his chest and he murmured soft nonsense words.

But he didn't promise to take her with him.

The fire had died down by the time he finally released her, and Flora felt drained. The exhaustion and fear and anger were still there, but the exhaustion was winning, dulling everything else to a vague throb in the back of her soul.

She'd needed the cry, aye.

But more, she'd needed his comfort.

Ducking hill, how she'd needed that.

How she craved it, even more.

"Get in the bedroll," he commanded, his tone clipped.

Her eyes flashed up to meet his, or where she guessed his eyes would be. "Why?" She was too wrung-out to be afraid or excited at the thought of sex with this man.

"Because ye need to sleep." Oh, mother's love, he was still angry. "I'll sit up and watch the fire."

She was already shaking her head but was uncertain why she was being stubborn. "Nay, 'tis yer bedroll. I'll sit up while *ye* sleep."

He watched her for a long moment, that helmeted head tipped to one side, before he blew out a breath. "Climb into the bedroll, Flora," he commanded again, only this time he sounded resigned. "I'll join ye."

Her breath caught, wondering if that meant her terrible seduction *had* worked. Mayhap something showed in her face, because he held up his hand, palm out.

"We're *sleeping*, Flora. If we're ever going to fook, 'twill be because *ye* want it, no' because of something ye think I can do for ye."

Keep me with ye.

But she was too exhausted to make sense of the jumble of emotions in her head and her heart, so instead of continuing to argue with him, Flora sank down onto the bedroll and pulled the heavy cloak atop her.

She watched through heavy eyelids as Payton built up the fire again, saw to the horse, then went outside the firelight to piss. He was out there a long time, and she was almost asleep by the time he returned.

He stepped over her and settled behind her so his back was to the rock, and placed his hand on her hip. When he tugged, her arse settled against his front—just the way they'd been all day—and the back of her head thwacked against the steel of his helm.

He slept with it on? Surely that wasn't a rule of the Hunters?

But Flora was too wrung out to ponder it.

"Go to sleep, lass," the man growled.

And, feeling warm and safe for the first time in almost a year, Flora obeyed.

CHAPTER 4

Well, fook.

Fook fook shite fook.

Payton was *not* in a good mood this morning.

He could blame it on the mutton—which always gave him gas—or the hard ground, not quite covered by the bedroll. He *could* blame it on the fact he had to sleep in the thrice-damned helmet, which *aye* had padding but not nearly enough to fooking *sleep in*.

However, he knew none of those were the true reason.

The true reason he was in such a bad mood this morning had naught to do with the sparse dinner or the hard ground or the helmet, and everything to do with the lithe and elfin beauty currently rubbing her backside against his aching cock as she slowly woke.

And the worst of it was, he couldn't tell if she was doing it on purpose.

Ye ought to have just taken her up on her offer last night. Ye could have flipped up yer kilt, shoved yer cock in her mouth, and been happy.

Nay, he wouldn't have been happy.

For one thing, as he'd told her, he wasn't going to *use* her that way. He didn't fook women who didn't want to be fooked, and Flora was clearly only offering her body in trade.

And secondly, Payton *couldn't* take her to MacIntyre Keep, as she asked.

He had enough to worry about at home—his reception would be a happy one, but full of nagging. His family would go bat shite if he returned home with a woman like Flora, and likely make assumptions he couldn't refute.

After all, in Flora's eyes at least, they *were* married.

By St. Bart's uvula, it had been hard to resist what she'd offered last night.

Aye, hard *being the operative word there.*

Knowing what torture awaited him if she slept in his arms, Payton had gone out into the darkness last night, ostensibly to piss. But he'd done more than that; he'd planted his arse against a large boulder, flipped up his kilt, and taken himself in hand.

He hadn't even needed to spit on his palm before he stroked himself—that's how painfully aroused he'd been. Nay, all it had taken was a few strokes, remembering the way she'd looked on her knees, her tits spilling from her bodice, and he was ready to come.

Payton had wrapped his fingers around the head of his cock and squeezed, imagining the feel of her lips around him, or her tight cunny.

With a muffled groan, he'd spurted hot seed across the Highland snow.

And after, he'd been ashamed.

Now he was paying for it; the hand-frigging had done naught, apparently, because he was rock hard again, almost painfully so, and Flora was grinning as she sat up.

Fook.

"Good morning, Payton," she announced, sending him a

smile as she stretched. "Is there time to break our fast before we leave, or are we in a hurry?"

Hell yes, he was in a hurry. He needed to get to the village and drop her off there, so he could start forgetting about her.

Flora would be safe there. Surely? The Abbot's reach wasn't that far, was it?

He rolled to his feet, wearing a frown beneath his helmet and doing his best to walk hunched over so he wouldn't embarrass himself with his tented kilt. The last thing he needed was for her to offer her body again—he wasn't certain he'd be strong enough to resist her a second time.

"Why are ye in such a cheerful mood?" he grumbled as he went to kick the fire into life again.

"Well, love a duck, Payton, it's shaping up to be a beautiful day, and I've slept better than I ever have."

Really?

He'd been miserable—well, nay, not quite. Actually, it had felt fooking amazing to hold her all night. Aye, her sweet little body had been pressed against his in all the right ways...he'd only been miserable because he'd been unable to *do* aught about it.

So, he scowled at her, although she couldn't see. "Why do ye talk like that?"

"Like what?" She looked up from rebraiding her hair.

"Love a duck. Son of a biscuit. What the frog." Actually, he found her way of cursing to be...endearing, he supposed, and he didn't want her to cease. But 'twas as good a distraction as any.

Luckily, she didn't seem to mind the question. Flora rose and began to roll up the blankets. "My father used to say those things. He once told me my mother didn't want him to curse around my younger brother and myself, so he started using those words instead. I just..." She shrugged without looking up. "Started using them as well."

"Oh," he grumbled, hoping he hadn't sparked some painful memories for her. What had happened to her father? How had she come to be at the Abbey?

"Why no' wear this today?"

He turned to find her holding out the warm cloak he'd given her, looking almost...shy?

"Nay, lass," he said gruffly, shaking his head. "'Twas a gift. 'Twill keep ye warm."

"Oh." She didn't drop her arms. "But...if ye're wearing it..." She swallowed and met his eyes. "If 'tis wrapped around ye to keep ye warm, and I'm sitting in yer lap, then *ye'll* be keeping me warm."

The logic was sound. And he had to admit, his back had been chilly yesterday without the cloak. But...

He shook his head. "'Tis more important ye stay warm, Flora."

And those big, trusting hazel eyes blinked up at him. "Ye'll keep me warm. I ken it."

Which is why they ended up atop his horse, the cloak wrapped around his back, and Payton wrapped around *her.*

"Payton?" she asked, after only a few miles. "Why do ye keep yer helmet on still? Ye slept in it last night."

As if he needed a reminder. His right ear still ached from the pressure of the steel. "The King's Hunters wear it when we're on a mission," he explained gruffly. "It hides our features, makes us more uniform. Intimidating."

She hummed, and he wondered if *Flora* found it intimidating.

"But ye're nae longer on a mission, are ye?" she asked, burrowing deeper into the little pocket of warmth formed by his chest, arms, and the cloak. "Ye defeated those bandits easily."

Aye, but...

"I'm still on a mission." He knew he was being surly when

he uttered that lie.

Because, aye, 'twas a lie.

The reason he hadn't removed his helmet was he didn't want Flora to see him without it. Didn't want to watch the teasing laughter in her expression turn to pity and then revulsion when she saw the scar which had destroyed his face.

"I hardly think this is a mission, Payton," she announced cheerfully as she patted his arm. "*Monkey feathers*, we're married. 'Tis no' a mission from the King."

St. Bart's beard, she was in a good mood today! He shook his head. "We're no' married, lass, nae matter what ye *or* yer monkeys believe. Yer Abbot might be a holy man, but nae holy vows were spoken. Only those yer people believe in."

When he saw the teasing light in her eyes—they were blue today, but as he watched they faded to gray—dimmed, he cursed himself.

"I did no' believe, Sir Hunter," she said quietly, shifting in his arms until she was staring over the horse's head. "And he's no' *my* Abbot."

Well, fook.

He'd hurt her.

'Tis for the best. Tomorrow morn ye'll say yer goodbyes to her, and 'tis best she believes there's naught between ye two.

Aye. Aye, for the best.

The afternoon light was waning—they were only a few days away from the longest night of the year—when he finally saw the smoke from the village he remembered. The track they'd been following had turned into a road a few miles back, and Payton knew they were approaching a part of the Highlands which wasn't quite as remote as the area around the Abbey.

Flora had perked up with interest as they approached the village. He was used to the stares and whispers the helmet evoked, but 'twas clear she wasn't.

Still, she lifted her chin and stared right back at the villagers who pointed and murmured, and beneath the obscuring helm, Payton had to smile.

For a quiet man, he was certainly gaining plenty of attention.

At the village inn—and tavern, and whorehouse, judging from the commotion—he left the horse in the stables with a well-paid lad who agreed to care for the animal as if 'twas his own mother, and he led Flora inside.

'Twas a joy, a genuine joy, to watch her excitement as she tried to take in all the room had to offer. The men drinking, the harried barmaids, the smells and sounds and sights... To Payton, used to the colors and refinement of the royal court, the general, overarching theme of this inn was...*brown*. But it reminded him of the tavern in the village near MacIntyre Keep, where Daniel had taken him for his first whore, before he'd sworn his sword to the King, and his brother had taken vows.

And so, he smiled again.

For the second time today! It must be a record.

"Dinner," he growled, remembering his duty as he stepped up to the rotund man behind the counter. "And two rooms."

The inn keeper swiped up his coin with a nod and knocked his knuckles against a keg. "Dinner, aye, and ale on the house, Sir Hunter. But we've only the one room."

Payton nodded brusquely. "'Twill do."

Flora's touch on his arm had him turning. "We can share," she offered, almost shyly.

His instinct was to tell her—as he had last night—that she should take the comfort of the bed while he kept watch. But staring down at her, he noticed her blush, and realization struck.

She'd said that last night had been the best night's sleep she'd had. They'd been lying on the hard ground, with the December air harsh around them...and she'd slept well. In his arms.

So, he nodded again, not able to speak because there appeared to be something wrong with his throat. Something stuck in it, damned inconvenient…

"A bath, Sir Hunter?" The little round man offered. "Another coin will buy ye use of the tub, and all the hot water my girls can fetch up the stairs."

Payton swallowed and cocked his head toward Flora. "Well, lass? Would ye like a bath?"

And damn him if she didn't *light the fook up*.

Seriously.

Her eyes, which he'd thought lovely before, became downright incandescent as she gasped and smiled.

'Twas that same smile he'd fallen half in love with the first night, when she'd knelt at his feet during the celebration. When she'd learned he was going to MacIntyre land.

The smile which reached down into his chest and *squeezed*.

The smile which made him want to do everything he could for the rest of his life, just to continue seeing that joy on her face.

"Really, Payton?" she gasped again. "A bath for *me*?"

She made him feel like a thrice-damned *hero*.

So, of course he was in a rotten mood when he turned back to the innkeeper and growled, "Take the lass up to the room and pour her a hot bath. Extra soap. Aught else she wants." He slid another pair of coins across the counter. "I'll be back in time for dinner."

As he made his escape, he could feel her eyes on him.

Payton lingered in the stables as long as he could, taking the last empty stall for himself. He drew a fresh pail of water, turned his back to the world, and removed his helmet. By St. Bart's warts, the cold air felt good on his skin.

Aye, even on his scar.

He dunked his head into the pail and scrubbed as much of the dirt as he could from his face and torso. 'Twas invigorating, aye, and when he emerged from the stall, he felt…well, like a new man.

Which made it that much harder to lower the helmet over his head once more, hating the way his wet hair stuck to the padding, hating the confinement.

He'd never hated the helmet before; always, it had just been a symbol, part of his purpose for being.

Now? Why was he resenting it now?

Because ye're going up to the room ye have to share with Flora, thanks to yer own sense of nobility, when ye want naught more than to taste her on yer lips.

Och, aye, that was it.

But his nobility had naught to do with it; he'd sleep in her room tonight because she'd asked him to. Because it made her happy.

And although he'd known her a short time, something told Payton he'd move heaven and earth to keep Flora happy.

Fook. Ye dinnae even ken her clan name!

Mayhap that was something he would discover tonight.

Head down, grumbling to himself about how little he knew of the woman he suspected he was losing his heart to, Payton placed his palm against the door to the rented room and pushed it open…

Just in time to startle Flora, who was rising from the wooden tub.

Her back was to him, and she froze halfway through the motion of lifting her leg over the edge, as if uncertain if she should sink back into the water.

There was a time when Payton would've apologized, stepped back, closed the door, offered her another apology.

Or he would've crossed the room, swept her into his arms, claimed her lips with his.

But tonight...

The lash marks on her pale skin...

"I'll fooking kill him," Payton growled, his fingers curling white-knuckled around the hilt of his sword. "I'll make him wish he'd never been born."

Flora's eyes widened at his vow, then followed his gaze. When she realized he was staring at her back—and the welts which crisscrossed it—she shook her head and continued climbing out of the tub.

"Most of them are auld, Payton," she murmured, reaching for the length of linen someone had laid out as a towel. She kept her back to him as she dried herself, which unfortunately only allowed him a clearer view of her scars.

Her arse too, and he vowed he'd look at that in a moment.

He just couldn't drag his gaze away from her back.

Without looking, he reached out to slam the door shut, stepping closer to her. "That doesnae make it better."

"Nay, but there's naught to be done now," she offered in a calm tone. "I wasnae verra good at following the Abbot's instructions."

As if pulled by a string, Payton found himself crossing the room, reaching for her... Halting his fingers before they could caress her skin.

Flora was right; most of the scars were white and puckered, but a few of the welts were red and inflamed. She'd been beaten regularly. And recently.

"They're no' all auld," he rasped.

Gasping—mayhap at his nearness—she whirled about, saw him standing within arms' reach, and gasped again. She spun back around and hurried to wrap the large towel around herself.

Not before he got another tantalizing glimpse of her small breasts.

Her hands worked furiously in front of her, tucking and tying the cloth into place, although it left her shoulders and arms bare. "Nay, some are new. The day afore ye arrived—the day afore ye challenged the bandits—the Abbot disapproved of one of my opinions."

Good Christ.

Payton had thought the man "strange," but he was more than that. He was cruel, to treat his followers that way. Flora said she disagreed with the Abbot, and didn't follow all his teachings...so why did she live at the Abbey?

Payton blew out a breath and turned away.

There were some who thrived in strict environments, like religious orders. Flora might have joined, then realized she regretted the decision. He didn't know her well enough to ask.

He knew naught about her.

Payton *wanted* to envelop her in his arms again, to allow her to release her pain as she had last night, so he could hold it. He *ached* to take the pain from her...but instead, he crossed the room to where the serving maids had left the dinner and occupied himself pouring ale from a flagon into a mug.

When he turned, Flora was watching him warily and he was struck once more. This time, not by her pain, but by her...

"What?" she blurted.

"Ye're beautiful, lass," he managed, gaze raking her clean face, clean shoulders...clean knees and feet.

To his surprise, she burst into laughter. The tinkling sound was new and caused him to blink. He wanted to make her laugh again, but not dismissively.

"Ye are," he insisted. "I thought ye waifish and dirty..."

"Aye, and I was! The innkeeper took my gown and chemise for his wife to wash, and threatened it might have to be burned," she laughed, as she crossed to him to snatch the mug from his hand. *"Jiminy crickets*, I would no' *beautiful*, Payton, even if I were dressed as a queen."

Still chuckling, she sank down on the edge of the bed, cradling the mug. "But it feels *so wonderful* to finally be clean." Her gaze flicked to the tub. "I confess, the water is barely warm by now—I stayed in too long—but if ye want to make use of it, I can—I can wash yer back. Or I can go and leave ye some privacy."

She wasn't looking at him. In fact, she was pretending great interest in her ale.

"Jiminy crickets?" he repeated, amused, as he unbuckled his sword belt and placed it over the mantel.

With her shoulders bare like that, her blush was obvious. It climbed up her cheeks and down her throat, and Payton realized her skin was quite fair, now it had been scrubbed vigorously.

"It means..." she attempted to explain the nonsensical phrase, but he waved her off.

"Nay, lass, I'm only teasing." He'd crossed his arms in front of his chest, and now leaned a hip against the table. "I washed in the stables, and I can wait a day for a hot bath."

"When..." Green-gray eyes peeked up from under dark lashes. "When ye reach MacIntyre Castle? Yer home?" she asked quietly.

That's where she wanted to go. After seeing the marks on her back, Payton suddenly hated the thought of leaving her here in the village.

Where he couldn't protect her.

"Aye lass," he admitted quietly. "My home. I'll be welcomed with a huge celebration, likely, since Mam kens I'm on my way, and I'll enjoy a bath then."

Her expression turned a little wistful. "That must be wonderful. To be welcomed like that..."

Was it? Frowning, he used one of his booted feet to snag the only chair standing before the table and dragged it closer. As he sat, he considered.

"I suppose it could be. My family is…enthusiastic. *Loud*." His lips twitched beneath his helm. "I prefer the quiet, and being alone."

"Being alone isnae all that fabulous," she offered softly.

"Nay, I can see that. I have friends among the King's Hunters, of course, and they've kept me company."

As he spoke, he served some of the steaming stew into a bowl, added a spoon, and leaned across the table to pass it to her. "But my family is different."

"Different, how?" she asked as she scooped up the dinner.

And since she seemed genuinely interested, he told her.

He told her about his friends among the Hunters—Barclay and Evander, who'd recently found love and retired, and Craig, the newcomer who was built like an ox—and some of the missions they'd been on. He spoke of his commander, Drummond Kennedy, a man who was even quieter than Payton himself, who valued order and control and refused to allow anyone close to him.

It seemed natural to sit there in the small room with the cheerful, crackling fire and speak of his past to this woman. She finished one bowl and started on another, and he tipped his helmet back far enough to partake in the thick brown bread and butter and ale. And still he talked.

He told her of his parents, who fought as fiercely as they loved, and their pride in their eldest son, who'd made Payton an uncle twice over already. He told Flora of the tower house and the adjoining holding Da had put aside for him, which his older brother Daniel was now overseeing, and he told her of his sisters.

"They sound lovely," she finally admitted as she tucked her feet up under her on the bed and placed the empty bowl on the table. "But I can understand how ye might be overwhelmed by them if ye're used to only the company of men—and a few of them, at that."

"Aye, overwhelming. 'Tis a good word for them, lass," he admitted. "I have no' been home in many months—since my aulder sister's wedding last summer—and my mother believes I'm avoiding them."

He *was* avoiding them, but he wasn't going to admit that to the woman who'd borne him.

Flora had twisted her hands in her lap and was now staring down at them. "So…if ye havenae been home in so long, ye… dinnae ken much of what's going on there?"

'Twas the way she asked it—meekly, haltingly—which caught his attention and raised his suspicions. "Why does it matter?"

"If there was…a person…living, mayhap, at yer family's holding. A *new* person…" She peeked up at him. "Ye wouldnae ken of him?"

Him?

Something verra like jealousy flared in Payton's chest. "Who do ye seek?" he growled.

When she shrugged one shoulder, the towel hitched, and she grabbed for the knot she'd made. "If I tell ye…"

She bit down on her lower lip, and Payton couldn't seem to drag his gaze away from that spot.

"Aye?"

"Please, Payton." She raised her eyes fully to his. "I have to ken if he's there. Lenny. My brother. That's why ye *must* take me with ye, *please*."

Her *brother*?

"Yer brother is at my family's keep?"

"I dinnae ken!" In her haste to make him understand, Flora leaned forward, her hair—still wet from the bath—cascading around her shoulders. "In the warmer months, the Abbey had a devotee join from MacIntyre land. I dinnae ken if he was a

MacIntyre—the Abbot makes everyone forswear their clan names and declare loyalty to *him*."

The *bastard*.

Flora took a deep breath, and he was startled to see her eyes were shining. Not from excitement, but...tears?

"I was in the kitchens, preparing one of the communal dinners, when I overheard him speaking to another about a 'witch child' who'd recently come to live in his auld village. He spoke of the lad having different-colored eyes, just like Lenny."

Sniffing, she sat back on the mattress. "'Tis no' much to go on, but...Lenny is a quiet lad of ten, with one blue eye and one brown. If there's a chance my brother is at MacIntyre Castle, I have to go there and see for myself."

Fook.

She *did*.

"St. Bart's eardrums, lass," he sighed as he scrubbed a hand across his face.

Or at least...*attempted* to. The damned helmet got in the way. *Again*.

He couldn't leave Flora here in this village as he'd intended. Not when there was a chance the Abbot could find her and hurt her again. He needed to have her nearby, so he could protect her if that were the case.

And now he understood her desperation for reaching MacIntyre lands...he couldn't deny her.

He'd take her home with him tomorrow.

Decided, he raised his chin...to find her staring at him, head cocked to one side, and a small grin on her lips. "What?"

Ignoring his defensive tone, she unfolded her legs and stood. "Do ye ken, ye do that when ye're thinking, or ye're frustrated?"

"Do what?" he asked, although he wasn't focused on her words...not when he'd caught a tantalizing glimpse of thigh as she crossed to stand before him.

She was smiling now as she came to a stop in front of him. "Ye try to rub yer face, but the helmet doesnae allow it. Ye said ye wear it whenever ye're on a mission, but 'tis obvious ye're no' used to wearing it nonstop."

Unbidden, Payton's hands curled into fists where they rested atop his thighs. She was close enough he could reach out and hold her. Pull her into his lap. Bury his face between her small breasts. *Taste her.*

"Will ye remove it, Sir Hunter?" she whispered, standing over him. "No' just for me, but for yerself, as well?"

St. Bart's bellybutton! She was so damned soft and sweet and…

Payton *wanted* to remove the helmet.

That's what it came down to.

He didn't want to wear the thing right now.

And besides…if he was going to take her to his home tomorrow, she'd see him without the helm then. He always removed it afore entering MacIntyre land, to remind himself he wasn't there on King's business.

If she was going to see him without it…might as well be now.

Her small hands were already on the steel and she was just waiting for his approval.

His voice harsh, he whispered, "Go ahead."

Slowly, reverently, she lifted his helmet.

Payton realized he was holding his breath, waiting for her gaze to land on the scar which had destroyed his visage. Waiting for her to recoil in revulsion—or worse, pity.

But…

Flora's eyes *had* gone right to the scar, and aye, her breath had hitched for a moment. But then her gaze caressed his jaw, his hairline, his whole ear on the right side, and finally…landed on his eyes.

Her gaze met his, and slowly, her smile bloomed again.

The beauty of that smile—crooked teeth and all—punched him right in the gut.

Without looking, she placed the helmet on the table, freeing her hands. She reached for him, her fingertips caressing his ruined cheek before cupping his jaw.

Then she leaned toward him. "Thank ye, Payton," she whispered, a moment before her lips brushed his.

Payton broke.

His control broke.

With a growl, he reached for her hips, pulling her down into his lap, as their lips crushed together. 'Twas joyous, aye, but also desperate, as if a dam had broken somewhere upstream, and there was naught they could do but ride this out.

His tongue dragged across her lower lip, the way he'd been aching to do since that first night, and her lips parted on a small whimper.

'Twas obvious she was new at this, but an eager learner, and he caught her little gasps of pleasure and matched them.

But as her arms settled around his neck and she squirmed against his arousal, a dim part of Payton remembered he couldn't take this too far. Last night, she'd offered him bliss, but only as a bribe.

Was that what she was doing now?

With a gasp, he pulled away, planting his forehead against hers and trying to control his breathing. "Christ, lass," he muttered, angry at himself for losing control.

She was breathing just as heavily as he was, her fingers playing with the hair at the back of his neck.

How was he going to resist her?

Swallowing, Payton stood, lifting her from his lap and placing her away from him. When she swayed, he grabbed her, telling himself he did it only to protect her, and knowing 'twas a lie.

Flora blinked up at him, her eyes hazy with desire, her lips swollen, and he had to fight the urge to crow with pride that he'd finally tasted her. Had to fight the urge to do it again.

"I'll take ye," he muttered, looking away. "Tomorrow. To MacIntyre Castle. I'll take ye with me."

And all it had cost her was one kiss.

Her happy little gasp was almost muffled by the way she snaked her arms around his waist and pressed her cheek to his chest. "Thank ye, Payton," she whispered again, squeezing him. "Will ye stay with me tonight? Just—" She hesitated. "Sleeping, I mean. Like last night. Holding…"

He shouldn't.

He wouldn't.

He did.

"Aye, lass," he agreed on a sigh, knowing he was damned to another night of torture and not hating it. "Aye."

He wasn't going to let her go.

CHAPTER 5

Flora's heart and mind were all in a jumble.

This morning, she'd woken in Payton's arms again, rested and comfortable and warm, while he...he was scowling. And this time, she could actually *see* the scowl, which somehow made it worse than having to guess.

He said little to her as they prepared to start their journey, and despite sleeping well—a real bed!—the night before, Flora realized she'd been on edge all morning, waiting for him to tell her he'd changed his mind. Waiting to hear he *wouldn't* be taking her to MacIntyre Castle to search for her brother.

Mayhap because she'd offered him no more than a kiss last night.

But...but that kiss.

That kiss.

Flora *ached*, just remembering that kiss. The way her breasts had tingled when he'd pulled her lower lip between his teeth... the way she'd had to clench her thighs together to attempt to assuage the ache in her core.

If he'd wanted more, she would have gladly offered.

But *Payton* was the one to pull away, to push her aside. He was the one to call a halt.

And she wasn't certain what to think of that.

He hadn't forbidden her from continuing the journey, and in fact lifted her into the saddle himself without speaking. His silence felt…awkward. Uncomfortable. They traveled most of the morning with minimal conversation, and after their noon stop, she'd had enough.

'Twas awkward, but Flora twisted around in her spot in Payton's lap to stare up at him. She wasn't certain how to start a conversation, but looking at him was just as nice, frankly.

She'd be lying if she said he was handsome; disfigured was a more accurate description. Some long-ago battle had nearly cost him his life; the scar stretched from one side of his face to the other. His left ear appeared to have been mangled by the blade, but he wore his dark hair long enough to cover it. The bridge of his nose was also bisected, and his right browbone.

'Twas a miracle both of his eyes were still intact, frankly.

But those eyes…

Those eyes were a fascinatingly warm color, a light brown with a darker rim, which made her want to stare into them for hours. And his lips were plump—far more beautiful than a man's lips had any right to be.

Last night, she'd tasted those lips, and she wanted to do it again.

"What?" he finally barked, his gaze locked on the road ahead.

She shrugged, pleased he'd finally spoken. "I like looking at ye."

When he scoffed, one side of those beautiful lips curled cruelly. "There's nae need to lie, lass, I'm taking ye to MacIntyre Castle."

A little hurt, Flora shifted again so she could face him more squarely. "I'm no' lying. I havenae been allowed to see yer face, and now I want to look at it."

"Nay, ye dinnae," he grumbled, even as he reached for her hips with his free hand and tried to turn her back around.

"Why is that so hard to believe?" She resisted his efforts to move her, and when she squirmed back again, felt a growing hardness against her hip. *Ah*. "Can I no' be curious?"

"Och, I'm used to curious stares," he muttered, his gaze very carefully *not* dropping to her. "I just dinnae like them."

"Because of yer scar?"

Finally he glanced at her, just briefly, before rolling his eyes. "Of course because of the bloody scar, lass."

"Ye shouldnae mind it." 'Twas difficult to manage, but Flora reached up to cup his cheek, just as she'd done last night, when she thanked him for removing the helmet for her. "'Tis just part of who ye are. Ye're handsome—"

"Nay, I'm no'," he muttered, snatching her hand from his face.

He didn't release it.

"I seem to recall ye called me beautiful yesterday. So, I get to call ye handsome today."

Payton didn't look at her, but one corner of his lips twitched. "Go to sleep, Flora."

She blinked. "I'm no' sleepy."

"Ye should rest. Tonight there'll be a celebration and we'll have to stay up late. If I ken Mam, we'll have to fetch the Yule log tomorrow or the next day, and then the *real* celebration starts. Ye should rest now."

She didn't want to rest; she wanted to keep looking at Payton.

But...his thumb was making small circles against the back of her hand. And she *was* quite cozy...

His gaze flicked down to hers once more. "If ye dinnae, I'll be forced to kiss ye again."

Well, with *that* kind of incentive... "Then I'll stare at ye all day."

He blew out a breath, but aye, there was a hint of a smile when he said, "Go the fook to sleep."

Grinning, she snuggled down in his arms and obeyed.

In the circle of his arms, with his cloak wrapped around both of them, she was safe and warm and oh-so-comfortable...

She woke up with her face plastered to his chest, drooling all over him.

Flora started, jerking upright and bringing her hand to her mouth to try to surreptitiously wipe the sticky saliva away.

"Oh good."

At the sound of his voice, she startled again and looked up at him guiltily, the back of her hand still pressed to her chin. He was staring straight ahead, his shoulders rocking slightly with the movement of the horse, but his lips were curled.

Without looking down at her, Payton said conversationally, "If ye slept any longer, I was afraid I'd have to change shirts afore I arrived home."

Scowling, Flora shifted her gaze to his shirt, where—aye—there *was* a big wet spot. Defensively, she pushed herself away from his chest and finished wiping her mouth. "'Tis no' so bad."

"I had a dog once, as a lad, who drooled like that when he slept. Of course, I rarely let him sleep *on* me, but ye do a fair—"

She smacked his arm to halt his teasing. "A gentleman is no' supposed to notice when a lady does something like that."

"What? Drool? How about fart? Can I notice when ye fart?"

"Ladies dinnae fart." She sniffed haughtily and sat straighter. "We release cute little pink puffballs."

"And sweat?" She could hear the teasing in his voice.

She'd never been a lady in her life. "We dinnae do aught as coarse as *sweat*, Sir Hunter. We glisten."

He snorted, and she felt her lips twitch as well.

"Well, lass, guess I dinnae have much interest in *ladies* then. Spoiled twits, mostly, concerned only with fashion and their husband's wealth. Some are cruel, many ready to cuckold their husband when he's away at battle." Payton lowered his head until his mouth was even with her ear. "And they never, ever *sweat*."

Flora swallowed. "I-I am a crofter's daughter, Sir Hunter. I sweat."

He inhaled, deeply. Was he...was he *sniffing* her?

"I do too, lass. I'm nae gentleman."

The way he said it sent little shivers down her spine.

"And Flora?"

"Aye?" she breathed.

"I notice *everything* about ye."

Oh.

Well.

It almost made drooling all over him worth it.

Soon enough, he announced they were approaching MacIntyre Castle, and she forgot the tingles on her spine from his touch. Well, not-quite-forgot, because he was there, a constant presence at her back and in her mind...but she sat up straighter and began to look around in excitement.

A they passed each crofter's hut, she peered about, looking for signs of Lenny. When they reached the village where passing MacIntyres greeted the laird's son with shouts of welcome, she craned her head, hoping for a glimpse of a tow-headed lad.

When they crossed into the castle bailey, she couldn't help slumping against Payton's chest in disappointment.

"Easy, lass," he murmured, even as he directed the horse toward the stables. "If he's here, we'll find him. I swear."

The vow *did* calm her racing heart. That, and the knowledge he understood her so well.

But all of that calmness went right to shite when he lifted her down from the horse, tucked her hand in his, and headed for the main steps. Because standing on the steps, leading up to the large door, was a woman.

CAROLINE LEE

Nay, a *lady*.

She was small—almost as small as Flora herself, and covered head to toe in a beautiful cloak of deep red, with white fur at the collar. Her hair had once been dark, but was now streaked with gray, and she was beaming at them as if they were the answer to her prayers.

Nay. Not at *them*.

At Payton.

"My mother," he murmured under his breath as he led Flora forward. "Brace yerself."

Brace herself? But the woman smiling down at them was regal, and poised, and elegant. Everything Flora *wasn't*. Why would she need to—

"Payton, *sugarplum*, ye're home! At last!" the lady declared, pushing her expensive cloak out of the way to reach out her arms to her youngest son. "Oh, I've missed ye so much! Ye must promise no' to stay away so long, baby bear! Look at ye—grown another inch at least!"

As Payton lifted her into his arms, she continued her monologue, without giving him a chance to respond. "And I see the King is feeding ye well enough, bless him. Are ye well? We'll have ye fattened up in nae time! Put me down, my wee cub, and give me a kiss."

Payton obediently lowered her to her feet—she *was* taller than Flora, but not by much—and placed a kiss on her offered cheek, only to have his shoulder swatted good-naturedly as the woman pulled him in for another hug.

"Och, 'tis *so good* to have ye back at last! And none of this running off again as soon as the holiday is over, with claims the King needs ye. His Majesty can do without ye for a month or two—aye, I said it, Pay-pay, dinnae argue with me, a month or two! Ye can see to yer family and yer holdings and oh, heavens, this is just so wonderful to have ye here, my little sweetmeat!"

"Aye, Mam," Payton said with a straight face, as he allowed

himself to be pulled up the stairs and into the castle. The look he shot over his shoulder at Flora said *See?*

His mother continued to chatter—and call him adorably ridiculous names—all the way into the great hall. When she finally halted and began calling for servants to fetch her husband and the rest of the family, Flora breathed out a sigh of relief.

She'd been trailing behind Payton, trying not to be overwhelmed, and uncertain where she should go and what she should do. She wasn't a guest here, not exactly. Not when *she'd* been the one to force her presence on him. 'Twould likely be best to slip away to the servants' quarters and beg for a crust of bread and a corner to curl up in, but the heat from the huge hearth in the center of the great hall was ducking close to intoxicating.

A few more minutes...

"Someone fetch the steward! I want a runner sent to the tower house calling Daniel home. Puir lad, he's desperate to have his own congregation, and will be pleased to turn the responsibilities over to ye once more—at least two months home this time, Pay-pay, dinnae dare to deny yer mother this!" She waggled a finger under her son's nose. "Och, there's Anna! Anna, Payton's finally home. Honeybear, ye remember yer sister-in-law, Lady Anna? And my favorite grandson Simon, is he no' adorable!" Under her breath she muttered, "Anna's increasing again, say naught about food in her presence. Simon, dumpling, come to Nanny!"

Lady MacIntyre had finally stopped talking long enough to take a breath, so Payton grabbed her by the hand afore she could reach for the toddler. "Mam, I ken I'll see everyone at the meal tonight. For now, we'd like to get cleaned up, aye?"

For the first time, his mother *and* sister-in-law switched their attention to Flora, who shrank a little at the scrutiny. She hadn't expected *Payton* to draw attention to her.

CAROLINE LEE

Lady MacIntyre's gaze lingered on Flora's skinny calves, visible beneath her borrowed, too-short woolen gown which should have been cut up for scraps years ago. "Why are ye no' wearing shoes, lassie? Are those rags tied to yer feet? Why are the rags tied to yer feet? Who are ye, and why are ye with my son?"

Lady Anna bounced her bairn and rolled her eyes. "Agnes, let the wench speak. Clearly Payton has brought home his paramour and expects ye to house her."

His mother was already nodding—and Flora flushing in embarrassment—when Payton introduced her. "Mam, Anna, this is Flora. Flora, my mother, Lady Agnes MacIntyre, and my aulder brother's wife, Lady Anna."

Flora did her best to curtsey, given the brevity of the sack she wore. She kept her gaze down and hoped she could escape before the ladies made further assumptions.

Lady MacIntyre didn't acknowledge the greeting, but merely clucked at her son. "Is Anna right, sugarplum? Ye brought yer lover home with ye for Hogmanay? And ye couldnae even bother buying her shoes, much less a dress which doesnae look as if it belongs on a donkey? Ye thought to shame our household such?" She sighed hugely but didn't give him a chance to say aught before she waved her hand dismissively. "And I suppose ye'll want to share a chamber with her, which is good, because we dinnae have extra space, what with yer brother and yer sister Clare's family—"

"Mam," Payton interrupted, "Flora is my wife."

'Twas almost gratifying to see the way the woman's mouth dropped open, for once not a single sound emerging. And one day, Flora knew she would pull out that memory and hold it up to the light and truly examine it, treasure it.

For now, however, she was busy staring, agape, at Payton as well.

He'd called her his *wife*.

He'd announced it in front of his mother, his family, *everyone*.

She was already shaking her head when he reached out and took her hand, pulling her gently up against him and tucking her into his side.

And Flora still hadn't managed to draw a full breath.

He'd claimed her. As *his*. When he didn't believe they were married—didn't believe the Abbot had any power. He'd *told* her that...hadn't he?

But, proving his mother wasn't going to let aught keep her quiet for too long, Lady Agnes snapped her mouth shut, shook her head briskly, then nodded.

"Well. Then." She took a deep breath. "I apologize for my rudeness, Lady Flora. Ye can imagine our surprise—from my pumpkin who has always claimed he'll never marry! I just didnae expect him to bring home a *wife*!" As she spoke, she became more animated—more *excited*? "Come, Lady Flora, ye must allow me—"

One *lady* she could let pass, but Flora couldn't allow these people to continue to call her such. "Not *lady*, milady," she offered quietly, with another little curtsey. "Just Flora."

She was a simple crofter's daughter. She'd never be a lady in a castle like this one.

To her surprise, 'twas Payton's sister-in-law Anna who answered with a soft smile. "When ye married our Payton, ye became a lady, Flora. But please, call me Anna." She offered a hand. "My feet have flattened with each pregnancy, and I have a pair of sturdy winter shoes ye might have. Never mind shaming our household; the fact Payton allowed ye to travel in such style shames *ye*."

Swallowing, Flora glanced at Payton, but he offered no more help than a small nod. She wanted to defend him to his family, to explain who she was and why she looked this way, but with that single announcement, he'd proven she really didn't understand what was going on.

So, she put her hand in Anna's and allowed the lovely woman to pull her toward the stairs, apologizing for her earlier assumption.

What followed was a strange few hours for a lass raised in a simple hut. For one thing, Lady Anna—who really was quite nice, once she relaxed—had approximately eight dozen servants, constantly coming in and out of her chambers. She was able to carry on multiple conversations at once—perhaps she'd learned that from her mother-in-law—about the upcoming celebrations, her two bairns and the one on the way, and the wardrobe Flora was to have.

Flora did her best to keep up, but kept insisting she didn't need any special treatment. A second bath? It felt positively gluttonous, and more than a little uncomfortable, with all the women—servants and Anna alike—flitting about the room. They exclaimed over her scarred back, but Flora quickly made up a story about falling in a briar patch, because she didn't have the energy to explain the Abbey.

"Och, of course!" Anna exclaimed. "That would explain what happened to yer gown and hose and shoes as well, ye puir lassie. They were likely shredded, along with yer skin. Well, dinnae fash, we'll get ye cleaned up and dressed as befitting the wife of a laird's son, soon enough."

Anna MacIntyre was a force to be reckoned with, and more than a little gullible, was she not?

Several times, Flora tried to bring up Lenny, to ask if anyone had seen a lad like him...but she was brushed off or ignored. 'Twas frustrating, and she found herself wondering what Payton was doing.

After a few days on the road with him—the peace and quiet—this hustle and bustle felt strange.

At last, Anna declared her ready to meet the rest of the

family, and Flora had to admit...she *felt* like a lady. Her hair had been pulled and brushed and pinned up, and she wore a beautiful gown of green silk.

Her hands were still callused, her back was still raw, her skin was still chapped, her teeth too crooked, and her features too plain...but from afar, she might pass as a lady. She certainly looked ready to face Payton's family.

What had she gotten herself into?

Payton himself met her at the bottom of the stairs, and the way his gaze raked her from head to toe made her cheeks heat. He merely offered her his arm and turned toward the great hall...but when no one else was around, he bent close enough to whisper, "How are the shoes?"

Somehow, she was pleased he hadn't offered her empty compliments. "They fit perfectly, to my surprise," she murmured back. "Yer sister-in-law likes to take command, for certes."

"She gets that from Mam. My sisters are just as bad." His warm brown gaze flicked down to hers. "Are ye ready?"

She took a deep breath. "As ready as I'll ever be."

"Well then, *wife*, let's start with my Da."

Still reeling from that casual term—was he teasing her?—Flora allowed herself to be introduced to Payton's family.

They were just as loud, just as overwhelming as he described, and the meal was *exhausting*.

Toast after toast was given to Payton's return, and his *happy marriage*, and with each one, Flora felt herself sinking deeper and deeper into the bench seat. If Payton hadn't been beside her—hadn't been answering each toast with a good-natured salute and smile, while allowing her to clutch his hand below the table—she wasn't certain what she would've done.

As 'twas, she wondered if she was the only one who noticed the tension around his eyes.

Why was he letting his family think they were married?

CAROLINE LEE

The first time someone had addressed her as Payton's wife, he should've stood and told the truth. They were never going to forgive him for this mockery.

His brother Daniel—the middle son, already ordained with a small flock to care for at the tower house—was the only one who Flora thought might suspect something. Oh, he'd bowed nicely enough, but throughout the dinner, he studied the pair of them thoughtfully, and looked as if he had something he wanted to say.

He never did, but *fudge buckets*, by the end of the meal, Flora thought she might explode from the tension.

Which would be messy.

When Payton stood and offered his hand, she took it like a lifeline, not ashamed to be seen as weak. *Shitake mushrooms*, she wasn't sure of half the things he said to extricate themselves from that situation, but finally—*finally*—they were walking away from the revelry, and Flora felt as if she could breathe again.

"Just a few more minutes," he murmured at her side. "Mam has aired out my auld chambers, I hope ye dinnae mind sharing with me?"

She snorted. "Ye might've asked that afore ye allowed everyone to think we were married."

He didn't reply, and when she glanced up at him, 'twas to see his jaw tight and his gaze locked on the corridor ahead.

Was he not going to explain *why* he'd made the claim?

Did it matter?

Aye, it matters! Ye dinnae want to be married to him! Ye're only here—with him!—to find Lenny!

But...was that the truth?

"Milady?"

The call came from behind, and Flora jumped, terrified she was about to be dragged back to the crowded celebration down in the great hall.

But the lass who hurried toward them looked younger than Flora herself, and when she stopped before them, she offered a quick curtsey.

"I'm sorry to be bothering ye, milord, milady, but I tended to ye in yer bath earlier, Lady Flora."

Payton shot her an amused glance. "Another bath?"

She elbowed him. "Ye had one, did ye no'? Yer hair is all shiny and ye smell delightful."

"Ye noticed that?" Something in his gaze changed—heat, promise, lust—and she realized what she'd admitted.

Trying to control her blush, she turned back to the serving lass. "Aye," Flora managed. "I remember ye. Lizzie, aye?"

"Aye, milady." The lass bobbed again. "I heard ye asking about a laddie, one with mismatched eyes?"

Flora's heart began to thunder in her chest, and suddenly she couldn't force her tongue to work. Couldn't do more than gape at the servant.

'Twas Payton who answered. "Aye, with pale hair. His name is Lenny." He stepped forward eagerly. "Do ye have news of such a lad?"

The girl held up one finger and turned back down the corridor. "I dinnae ken his name, milord," she called as she reached the corner. "Because he hasnae spoken since he arrived, but this lad has been working in the stables for months now."

With that, she tugged on a small arm, standing just out of sight, and Flora felt the sun come out.

"Lenny," she gasped, as her brother stepped around the corner and met her eyes.

He blinked at her, and for one horrible moment, she worried he didn't know her. What had the lass said—he hadn't spoken? Nay, that wasn't right. Her brother could—

"Flora?"

His whisper carried, and as the servant girl gasped and

made the sign of the cross, Flora pulled away from Payton and lunged for her little brother.

In the center of the corridor, they slammed into one another, the impact wrenching a sob from her lips. Lenny buried his face against her shoulder—he'd grown in the months since she'd seen him—and she wrapped her arms around him, holding him tight.

The questions of the last minutes, the stress of the meal, the horrors of the last months...they all melted away. Whatever challenges she'd faced, she would face again, for this moment.

Lenny was here, and he was safe.

"I thought ye were dead," he muttered, barely heard above her pulse.

"I'm no'," she gasped, squeezing him tighter and rocking back and forth. "I'm no'. I've been trying to reach ye—to find ye. For so long, Lenny. But I'm here."

"Ye're here," he sniffed, and she felt his fingers digging into her back.

Through her tears, she twisted and met Payton's eyes over her brother's mop of blond hair. This man was the reason she'd been reunited with her brother, this wonderful man.

He was standing there, his arms crossed in front of his chest, still wearing the King's colors, watching her hug Lenny. There was something in his expression...something she couldn't identify.

She owed this man so much, and suddenly, the questions from earlier—why he'd made the claim to his family, why he'd allowed her to be treated as his wife—didn't matter. She owed him her heart and her soul.

"Thank ye," she breathed, so quietly she doubted he heard her.

But when he nodded solemnly, she saw the glint of moisture in his eyes, and knew he was glad for her.

CHAPTER 6

PAYTON TRIED to be quiet as he pushed open the door to the corridor. Normally it wouldn't matter—not this long after dawn, when the household was likely awake and bustling already—but Flora was still asleep, and he didn't want to wake her.

Last night had been hard on her, between the celebration, his family, and finding her brother. Nay, *finding* Lenny hadn't been difficult—it had been bloody near miraculous. But her emotions had been so wrung out, between the tears and tension, that Payton had eventually scooped her up and tucked her in, and the lad hadn't objected.

Sleeping with her in his arms was a special, wonderful kind of torture.

Not just because apparently she liked to roll and flop about. And she drooled whenever her cheek landed on his shoulder, which he thought was just adorable.

Gross, aye, but adorable. It made her seem...more human. Less like one of those primped and proper ladies at court, and more...*Flora*.

He was thinking of her—and smiling—when he realized the

door he was pushing open was bumping against something. He tried again. And a third time.

The fourth time, he just *pushed*, then squeezed through the gap and peered around the door.

A very irritated-looking Lenny was sitting on his arse, his knees pulled up and his arms wrapped around them, glaring up at Payton.

"Och, lad, I'm sorry. I dinnae realize ye were sitting there." Keeping watch, mayhap? Payton offered his hand. "Did ye sleep here all night?"

Lenny glared at his hand until Payton withdrew it. Uncertain how to handle the situation, the large man crossed to the opposite side of the corridor, pressed his back to the wall, and slowly crouched, until he was on the same level as the lad.

"Are ye hungry?" he ventured.

Flora's brother just continued to glare.

Sighing, Payton scrubbed his hand over his face, then dropped his elbows to his knees. The lad must be scared of his ruined face. He *knew* 'twas horrific enough to send small children running for safety, but he'd become used to people at home ignoring the scar, since he'd had it for so long.

It hadn't occurred to him the lad might object.

"I swear I'm nae monster, Lenny," he said quietly. "Just a man with a scar."

To his surprise, the lad blinked, looked startled, then shook his head.

If that wasn't the reason he wouldn't speak, what was it? The serving lass last night had said Lenny hadn't spoken at all, but Payton had *heard* the lad whisper to his sister...

"Would ye like to ken how I got it?" he asked gently.

Lenny hesitated, then slowly lowered his knees to sit cross-legged. And nodded.

Blowing out another breath, Payton shrugged and felt one corner of his lips curl wryly. "'Twas one of my first missions as a King's Hunter. Ye ken who those are? We're men who've sworn our swords to Their Majesties. More than that, we're..." How to explain? "We keep the King's peace. We enforce his laws. We travel all over Scotland, tracking down criminals or rumors of wrongdoing, and the King trusts us to set things right. 'Tis a powerful trust."

The lad was staring at him, wide-eyed. Payton wondered if he understood.

"My commander, Drummond Kennedy, believes the newest Hunters should have mentors, and he'd taken me under his wing, so to speak. There was a laird—a small holding up near the Sinclairs—who was rumored to have been cruel and unjust, hurting his people. His Majesty sent us to investigate, and we didnae need to have bothered, because the bastard—"

Payton bit off his words, wondering for the first time if the story was appropriate for a ten-year-old. But the lad was leaning forward, almost eagerly, and Payton remembered the kind of stories *he'd* liked when he'd been that age.

He shrugged. "The laird had his men attack us, while he himself wielded a wickedly long dagger, aimed for my commander's back. While Drum finished the rest of the men, I stepped in front of that blade." He tapped at his missing ear. "It could've taken my eye. Or my life. I ken 'tis ugly, but I'm lucky to be alive."

Lenny's mis-matched eyes were wide, staring at the place where Payton's left ear used to be. And...there wasn't fear in that gaze.

So, he just didn't speak to anyone besides Flora? Was that it? Somehow, it made Payton feel a bit better.

Pushing himself to his feet, Payton offered his hand again. "I'm going down to break my fast. Ye're welcome to come with me. Then, if ye want, I can take ye out to the training yard. 'Tis likely packed with snow, but I can show ye how the bastard came at me, if ye'd like."

When Payton had been his age, and a warrior offered him lessons in the blade? Payton would've walked over hot coals for that.

Sure enough, Lenny's expression lit up, and the lad eagerly reached for his hand.

"If ye'd like, lad, tonight ye can sleep in there with yer sister," Payton offered in a low voice. "That way ye dinnae have to watch over her. That's what ye were doing, aye?"

The boy hesitated, shooting a multi-colored glance at the door, afore nodding slowly. Ah. So, it *hadn't* been concern over Flora which had kept her brother out here all night. Likely *he'd* been the frightened one.

Well, either way, having to share a room with him would keep Payton from kissing Flora again.

No matter how much he wanted to taste her again, he wasn't going to push himself on her like that.

"Let's go eat, lad."

THE FOLLOWING DAYS weren't any calmer. In fact, as Payton's sisters and their families arrived, the Castle became more and more crowded. 'Twas as hectic as he remembered holidays as a child. But whereas he used to find the constant motion and gatherings *exciting*, now he was merely tired by them.

And strangely, it seemed as if Flora felt the same way.

Despite his best efforts, he rarely saw her during the days.

While Mam and Anna—and his sisters—pulled her into preparing for feasts and festivals, Da and the rest of the men kept Payton busy with questions and requests for help. He traveled to remote crofts, he helped repair roofs in the village, and he even agreed to do some sparring to help train the younger warriors.

The only good thing about these full days was that Lenny,

more often than not, tagged along beside him. Aye, the lad sat with his sister at mealtimes, but he seemed to enjoy Payton's company well enough.

Mayhap because Payton didn't expect the lad to speak.

He noticed other MacIntyres ignored Lenny completely or treated him as if he didn't understand basic things. But Payton knew the lad just didn't prefer to speak, and thus didn't push him. He still taught Flora's brother useful things, and assumed *that* was why the lad followed him about.

This was, of course, less appealing in the evenings, after the celebrations, when everyone would retire to their chambers... because, thanks to Payton's invitation, Lenny now slept in his chamber.

How in St. Bart's big toe had this happened?

A month ago, he'd been alone—other than his brothers-in-arms—and happy about it. Now he had a fake wife and a lad who wouldn't leave him be.

And why didn't he hate this new change?

A month ago, he'd been dreading returning home to the chaos and confusion and *noise*. Now...well, he still was uncomfortable, but he cherished the evenings, when he could finally sit and just *speak* with Flora, hearing about her day and what she'd learned.

They also spoke of other things; his time with the Hunters, her years with her father and Lenny on their farm.

But he didn't ask her about her time in the Abbey, and she didn't volunteer it. 'Twas obviously an uncomfortable topic, and he didn't want Lenny to learn more about the evil in the world.

Preparations for the Yule kept all the MacIntyres in high spirits and Payton had to admit there was something joyful about the occasion. On the day designated to choose the Yule log, he cornered Flora after she broke her fast.

"Come with us?" he asked, catching her hand.

Startled, Flora peered around him. "Ye're leaving the keep?"

"We're off to fetch the Yule log. Of course, Daniel has already scouted ahead and found a good choice, so the hunt itself will likely be boring. I'm just anxious to escape a bit, and thought ye might be too?"

Her shoulders slumped as she exhaled, but the look she shot him was pure gratefulness. "I'm supposed to learn how to make cheese today, but I would *love* to join ye. Let me go fetch my cloak."

"And I'll find Lenny. I think yer brother would enjoy the adventure too."

Was it his imagination, or did something like disappointment flicker across her features afore she turned to hurry up the stairs?

When she joined him in the courtyard later, his face split into a grin when he saw what she wore. "Gone to fetch yer cloak, eh?" he teased, tucked her arm in his. "Ye mean *my* cloak."

Indeed, she was bundled in the fur-lined cloak he'd given her the night they met.

"Oh?" Flora glanced down at herself in surprise. "And here's me thinking ye *gave* it to me. Ye found another cloak, I see?" She flicked the wool he'd wrapped around himself, eyes twinkling. "Now, tell me if ye expect me to learn how to ride a horse today. I've never ridden by myself, ye ken."

"Ye havenae?" he was surprised, he had to admit. Lenny had taken to the activity like a fish to water. "Well, then, lass, ye'll just have to ride with me."

Her grin told him that had been her goal all along. "Oh dear. Such a shame. I call shotgun!"

"What?" he asked as he followed her to where the horses were prancing about.

"That one," she announced, pointing. "I call it Shotgun. And I'm riding in front of ye."

"For a change," he muttered sarcastically, but he was grinning as he pulled her up into his lap.

Where she belonged.

When Lenny trotted out on the little pony Payton had assigned him, Flora gasped and made a show of clasping her hands to her cheeks. "Lenny, look how handsome ye are, riding a horse like a man!"

Her brother rolled his eyes, but Payton noticed he was flushed with happiness as they joined the caravan heading into the hills. He was careful to fall toward the back, and Lenny did the same, slowing their horses until the laughing, singing, and already-half-drunk crowd pulled away ahead of them.

When he could no longer hear them, Payton pulled his horse to a stop, tipped his head back, and took a deep breath. The air was so cold it burned his lungs, but he didn't mind. "This is more like it. Finally alone."

Flora snorted quietly. "We can leave ye be, Sir Hunter, if ye want to be alone."

"Nay, I—" When he saw the teasing twinkle in her eyes, Payton did some eye-rolling of his own. "Ye two dinnae count. I'd rather be alone *with* ye, than without ye," he declared, swinging down from the saddle, and reaching up to grasp her about her waist.

"Aye," she murmured, and he loved the way her cheeks pinked, although she met his gaze. "I feel the same way."

Her feet were on the ground—hard-packed snow, thanks to the merry-makers who'd gone before—but he kept his hands on her waist, trapping her between his body and the horse. For her part, Flora was still holding onto his shoulders, as if she didn't want to let him go either.

"Flora?" Lenny's voice caused her to startle. "Are ye married to Payton?"

Without releasing her, Payton turned, tucking her up

against his side as they faced her brother. The lad's head was tipped up, and he was glaring at *Payton*.

'Twas Flora who answered. "Why do ye ask that?"

"Because everyone at the castle says ye're married. But I'm no' stupid. I ken what goes on between a married couple. And...ye dinnae *act* married."

Lenny was still glaring mulishly at Payton, so he was the one who spoke. "How do ye ken what passes between a married couple, lad?"

The boy didn't answer, but continued to glare.

With a sigh, Payton glanced down at Flora. "Could ye please ask yer brother how he kens what passes between a married couple?"

Lips twitching, she nodded. "How do ye ken what passes between a married couple, Lenny?"

"I've been working—and sleeping—in the stables since last spring, Flora. Nae one notices me if I dinnae speak, and the men talk."

Ah.

Payton shrugged. "Well, lad, ye've been sharing a chamber with yer sister and me since the day after we arrived here."

Again, Lenny didn't answer.

Payton glanced at Flora, who pressed her lips together and turned back to her brother. "Lenny, Payton's right. Ye've been sleeping with us."

"And is that why he cannae do"—the lad flapped his hands about—"Whatever 'tis ye'd rather be doing together?"

St. Bart's nose hairs, this was an awkward conversation.

"Let's walk, eh?" he blurted, taking Flora's hand in his and tugging her into motion, even as he caught the horse's reins in his other hand. "Lenny, ye can handle that beastie?"

Of course, the boy didn't answer, but he trotted alongside Payton soon enough. The man glanced over at him; Lenny was frowning, his attention on the snow before him.

"Lenny, ye've been treated well since arriving at MacIntyre Castle?" he asked softly.

The lad glanced at him, then back at the snow, and finally nodded.

Och, well, at least he'd answer, if he didn't want to speak.

"Are ye sleeping with Flora to protect her, or because ye dinnae want to sleep elsewhere?"

The lad kept his gaze square on the snow.

Payton raised a brow at Flora, who sighed. "Lenny! Same question, only 'tis coming from me, aye?"

The boy shrugged. "I'm no' scared to sleep in the stables, if that's what ye're asking. I can leave ye two alone."

"'Tis no' that," she began gently. "Payton and I...we're no' really married. We're sort of..." She hesitated, then shook her head. "I dinnae ken. But we havenae been married by the church."

"Aye," Payton jumped in, "but my family thinks we're married, and I'll no' have yer sister shamed by announcing we're no'."

The stubborn set of Lenny's jaw reminded Payton of his sister. The lad kept his attention on Flora. "Why are ye pretending then? Why do ye no' want her shamed?"

Payton raised his brows, as his boots crunched over the packed snow. The lad was clearly desperate for the answer, but he was still pretending to speak only to Flora. When he looked over at the woman in question, Payton was surprised to find her staring up at him.

"I confess," she said quietly, rubbing her brow, "that I had the same question for ye, Payton. Things just became so...busy. And then Lenny was with us, and I didnae think ye wanted to have this conversation with him around..."

He *still* didn't.

The sun was shining, the air was crisp, and the snow glistened on the pine boughs. 'Twas far too beautiful a day to verbal vomit one's feelings all over the path.

Instead, he pointed to footprints on one side of the path. "Look, a hare's been through here. If we had a bow, we could catch supper."

"Flora," Lenny snapped, "tell yer pretend husband to stop changing the subject."

"Pretend husband," Flora echoed, "stop changing the subject."

Payton hummed. "A fat rabbit, roasted in its own juices. Mayhap with parsnips and carrots—"

"Payton!" blurted Lenny, who then winced. "I mean, Flora, does he *want* to be married to ye?"

"Payton." She nudged him with her hip as they strolled. "If ye dinnae want to be married to me, ye didnae have to announce to yer family that we *were*. I thought ye didnae believe the Abbot's ceremony was binding."

"I dinnae," he muttered under his breath. Then he exhaled—a cloud of vapor wrapping through his beard—and scrubbed a hand over his face. "I thought ye didnae either."

"Aye," she said carefully. "But I'm no' the one who told yer mother I was yer wife."

"And I'm wondering *why*," Lenny added on.

"Because!" Payton exploded, turning suddenly and reaching for Flora. If he'd thought about it at all, he would've said that he intended to grab her shoulders, mayhap to shake her into understanding. But somehow his hands went to her face, his hands cradling her jaw, his thumbs resting on her cheeks as he looked into her eyes.

"Because, lass," he rasped, watching those beautiful eyes shade from blue to green. "*Because*. I couldnae stand the thought of them thinking ye were less than ye are. I didnae want them to force ye away from MacIntyre land afore ye could find yer brother. I didnae want my mother to think ye were a servant—or worse, my leman!" He tugged her closer. "And I didnae want to be parted from ye."

Her lips had formed a little "oh" of surprise, but he didn't want to give her time to respond. Was afraid *how* she would respond.

Instead, he kissed her.

This wasn't the same kiss they'd shared in the inn, the night he'd showed her his face for the first time; that one had been hot and desperate, a fire he thought might consume him.

This kiss...

He tried to show her all the things he couldn't put into words. The feelings he couldn't even put into *thoughts*.

He tried to show her the way she made *him* feel, as if he was a hero. As if he mattered, even among his chaotic family. He tried to show her how she kept him calm and focused.

Judging from her little moan, and the way she leaned into him, it didn't quite work.

After a long moment, he became aware of noises behind him. Lenny apparently disapproved of the kiss, judging from the retching noises he was making. At least, Payton *hoped* they were mere noises, and the lad wasn't actually puking his breakfast up at the sight of two people in love—

What?

Payton pulled away, staring into hazel eyes, hazy with desire. *In love?* Was he in love with Flora? He'd known her for such a short time...

Stop fighting it. Ye're in love.

A smile surprised him, bursting across his lips with the suddenness of an autumn storm, and she smiled softly, shyly in response.

Ye love her, aye.

She'd offered herself to him once before. And everyone already thought them married... But he'd lived most of his adult life with a horrific scar across his face, and knew he was no prize. He'd wait.

He'd wait until *Flora* wanted him for *him*, not for what he could give her or do for her.

Her hand was pressed against his chest, and he wondered if she could feel how frantically it beat. For her.

A small throat cleared behind him. "Flora, all things considered," the lad announced, "tell Payton I think I'll find someplace else to sleep tonight."

CHAPTER 7

FLORA DIDN'T like the idea of her younger brother sleeping in the stables, but as it happened, his vow to move out of the chamber she'd been sharing with Payton didn't matter, because there was barely time for sleeping any longer.

When the MacIntyres Yuled, they Yuled *hard*.

Did ye just verb the noun "Yule"?

Aye, one could verb aught if one tried hard enough.

Like right there. Where ye verbed the noun "verb"?

Exactly.

Between the log-lighting, the merry-making, and the holy Masses, Flora felt strung-out, like a piece of catgut drying for a lute-string.

No' a flattering analogy.

In the days following that kiss in the forest, she barely had a moment alone with Payton, and when she did, they did little more than talk about their plans or their days. Och, at night, 'twas still wonderful to curl up in his arms to sleep, and sometimes they kissed...but more often than not, she was too tired to keep her eyes open, and he chuckled and pulled her up against him.

But when she wasn't with him, the memory of that kiss kept Flora flushed and smiling. Payton had said he hadn't wanted to be parted from her! That was why he'd lied to his family, told them they were married.

'Twas no holy vow or plan for the future...

But for now, 'twas good enough.

On the one hand, she couldn't wait for Hogmanay to be over, so she and Payton could have some peace and quiet together.

On the other hand, once the new year started, he was due back at court, at the King's side, fulfilling his role as a Hunter. She wasn't at all certain what that would mean for her place in his life, or if she'd even have one.

And on the third hand—this was getting out of hand—she couldn't wish the holidays to pass too quickly, because Lenny was so excited about them.

Their mother had died giving birth to the lad, so Flora—being so much older—had done what she could to ensure Lenny had a happy childhood...up until the bandit attack. But their Yule and Hogmanay celebrations had been simple, unlike the celebrations at MacIntyre Castle.

And Flora supposed she could put up with a little overstimulation and a sensual yearning she could use to grease axels, if it meant her little brother got a few more days of holiday happiness.

Besides, watching him eat his way through a Yule celebration was enough to make a pre-hibernation bear proud. Flora was certain the lad was plumper than he'd been a fortnight ago.

However, she was more than ready to make an escape, so when Payton suggested one, she calmly considered the implications and agreed.

Or rather, it went something like this:

"Fook this shite, Flora. I cannae hear myself think in this

chaos. Tomorrow I'm going to the tower house, just to check on things. Ye want to go with me?"

"Oh my lanta, *aye!* Duck it, I'm desperate!"

"Duck? Did ye just say 'duck', Flora?"

"I never mean 'duck'. Nae one ever means 'duck.' That must've been some sort of auto-correcting mistake."

Luckily, he just chuckled, instead of questioning her sleep-deprived ramblings.

Which is why, this morning, afore the sun was even fully up and while most of the rest of the castle was still asleep, Flora found herself wrapped in Payton's cloak—and Payton's arms— once more.

"Ye ken," he mused as they trotted through the quiet village. "One of these days I'm going to have to teach ye to ride."

"Why?" She squirmed in his lap, turning to wrap one arm around his middle and press her cheek to his chest. "When this is so much cozier?"

"Because, lass, I dinnae think my cock can stand too much more of this torture."

She *loved* that he was so open and frank with her about that sort of thing. She also loved that she could feel his thickness pressing against her hip and knew what it meant.

Today, she was determined to do something about it.

Tomorrow night was the longest night of the year, after all.

"Will we back in time for the Hogmanay celebrations?" she asked, nonchalantly.

He hummed and adjusted his hold on her, tucking the cloak —which he wore once more—more securely around them both. "Unless something dire happens at the tower house. We should get there this afternoon, since I'm no' interested in pushing this puir beastie too hard. Spend the night there, back to the castle tomorrow in time for the Hogmanay celebrations, God help us."

Since the last part was said on a sigh, Flora felt comfortable chuckling. "I confess, ye were right about yer family. They're nice, all of them...but *shine my shoes*, they are exhausting. I had to have an entire conversation with yer cousin Ellis about little green men, government conspiracies, and why we should wear special hats to keep our minds from being scanned. I dinnae even ken what tin foil *is*."

"Och, Christ, lass, I'm sorry. Ellis is...a handful. His mother is the one who gets drunk and starts spouting off hateful remarks about people who look different from her. But neither is as bad as my sister's husband, who thinks he kens all there is to ken about everything."

Shirt stain, she'd barely been able to last ten minutes with that arsehole! "I guess family gatherings are a trial, nae matter who yer family is."

Chuckling, Payton launched into a story about another family gathering—one which involved a lot of ale and a medical emergency—and then another. She shared stories of her simple holiday celebrations in her father's croft, and they both discussed possibilities for Lenny's future.

"He's a good lad with horses. And he'll make a fine warrior in a few years, as long as his training continues."

"Thank ye," she murmured, staring at his chin, "for giving him that opportunity. If we'd stayed on MacGregor land, I dinnae ken if he'd be given the choice. He would've taken over Da's croft, and that would be that. Now he has options, I suppose."

Although she'd never be *pleased* for the horror which had left her at the Abbey, at least Lenny had a future now, and she...

She had Payton.

For however long he was willing to be with her.

He cleared his throat, his arms tightening around her as the horse picked its way down a steep slope. "Will ye tell me, lass, how 'twas ye came to be at the Abbey and separated from Lenny?"

She was surprised he hadn't asked earlier, frankly.

"They came in the middle of the night," she whispered, transferring her gaze to the distant mountains. 'Twas easier than looking in his eyes. "I remember the smell of their torches. 'Twas early spring; we hadnae even begun the planting, the ground was still frozen. They...fired the thatch of our roof."

He said naught, but held himself as still as a statue.

"There was so much yelling and confusion," she continued. "Da ran out and I saw them cut him down. Right there in front of us, they just..." She shook her head, flinching again at the memory of the flash of reflected torchlight on the blade. "I held Lenny so he wouldnae see, but eventually the smoke was so bad we had to run outside too."

"What happened?" Payton's voice was little more than a rasp.

"They pulled us apart. I saw one of them hit Lenny with something—on his head. He fell and I screamed...that's all I remember."

Until she'd woken up, thrown over a horse, on her way to the Abbey.

Behind her, around her, Payton had stilled further, until she wasn't certain he was breathing. "Who did this?"

"Bandits." Finally, she forced herself to meet his eyes. "The same bandits who the Abbot requested help wiping out."

Payton's breath *whooshed* out all at once, and she felt his shoulders slump. "Then I'm glad I killed them. I should've made them suffer."

"Nay," she choked, then pressed her cheek to his shoulder once more. "They cannae hurt anyone again."

And ultimately, they were just acting under orders...

Apparently determined to cheer her, Payton made an effort to change the topic, launching into a list of possibilities for

Lenny in the coming years. She appreciated that he cared for her little brother and wanted what was best, but 'twas difficult to consider a future when she didn't know where *she'd* be.

Still, they chatted about naught much at all, and soon they were laughing again, and there were even a few kisses throughout the journey.

And when they arrived at the tower house—one of the MacIntyre border holdings, a stone tower surrounded by a pleasing wooden building—she actually gasped aloud.

"Love a duck, Payton, it's *lovely*!"

"Aye, 'tis." He seemed surprised, as if only just realizing. "I havenae been back here in a few years. I dinnae ken why Daniel has complained so much about being forced to live here."

Flora, who'd had the opportunity to befriend Payton's next-oldest brother, said, "I can. This holding is much smaller, aye? Look, there's only the stables and a few outbuildings. No' even a proper village. Daniel wants to return to the castle, where he can watch over the congregation and say Masses in the church yer grandfather built."

Lips twitching, Payton glanced down at her. "Aye, ye're right. He'll be much happier amid the hustle and bustle of the MacIntyres. But this place…"

He trailed off, and she twisted so she could look up at him.

He was smiling, a satisfied, wistful sort of grin as he looked around.

"This place could be a home," she whispered, still staring up at him.

He glanced down. "Aye, lass. It could. Would ye like a tour?"

Purple pickles, aye!

Flora didn't bother to hide her excitement as he showed her the tower house and introduced her to the couple who acted as the housekeeper and steward. The wife had hired a few of the local lassies as maids, and there was a gruff older man who was apparently the cook. He acted as if 'twas a waste of time to show them the kitchen, but Flora could hear the pride in his voice.

And after they'd toured the rest of the buildings, they sat down to a cozy, delicious dinner. Mayhap the cook *did* know what he was doing.

"So, what do ye think?" Payton asked, elbows on the table as he held a leg of fowl. "Of this place."

"'Tis *wonderful*," she admitted truthfully. "No' as overwhelming as yer home, and more welcoming. Nae offense."

He waved the chicken. "None taken. MacIntyre Castle was where I was born and where I grew up, but this place..." He looked around with a calculating eye, as if really seeing it for the first time. "Da set it aside for Daniel, and when it became obvious he was destined for the Church, granted it to me. *This will be my home when I retire from the King's Hunters.*"

"And..." Slowly, she placed her flagon back down on the simple table, not looking at Payton. "And when will that be?"

"Most Hunters retire when they marry if they have a place to support themselves and their families. I suppose I'm lucky to have someplace to go."

There was...*speculation* in his voice. Flora peeked at him from under her lashes, and saw him staring at the hearth, something like understanding dawning in his eyes.

"Are ye willing to give that up?" she asked quietly, hardly daring to breathe. "Being a King's Hunter?"

His gaze shifted to her, and she froze, caught by his stare. "I hadnae considered it."

"And now?"

The firelight caused shadows to flicker across his face, highlighting his strong jaw and sending shadows across the craggy scar. "I'm considering it."

What about me?

She wanted to ask it, but the moment was so tight with unspoken words, she didn't think she could.

Instead, she whispered, "Could...ye be happy here?"

"Aye." His answer was immediate, and his gaze didn't leave hers. "Could ye?"

Oh, *aye*.

She hadn't realized she'd said it out loud until his visage slowly softened into a smile.

"Have I shown ye the master's chambers yet?"

'Twas almost comical, the way they rushed up the stairs, holding hands and laughing like children.

The master's chamber was smaller than Payton's room at the castle, but still larger than the croft Flora had grown up in. A thick blanket covered the bed—tightly woven in the MacIntyre colors—and the cheery fire in the hearth warmed the room.

They came together in the center of the room, hands grasping and lips ready. She tugged at his shirt, and he groaned.

"Lass, wait," he managed, but Flora didn't *want* to wait. She stepped away from him and began scrabbling at the ties to her simple gown. She had her kirtle over her head and was rolling down her hose when he was still only unlacing his boots.

Hurry hurry hurry

She wanted to feel his touch on her skin. She wanted to taste him!

In just her chemise, she threw her arms around his neck once more. Payton, wearing only his kilt, seemed ill at ease.

"Are ye certain lass? Ye want...*this*?"

When he said that, his hand made a little gesture, a little jerk toward his face, and she wasn't quite certain what he meant. But the way his kilt was tenting in front of him told her what she needed to know.

"It seems *ye* do," she breathed, rubbing her hips back and forth. Each time his hardness came in contact with her core, her pulse jumped. "Come to me, Payton."

"Nay, I..." He broke off with a groan as she pulled him

toward the bed, and when they fell atop it, he wasn't complaining.

In fact, his kisses turned just as frantic as hers, and his hands...

When he cupped her breast through the linen of her chemise—finer than aught she'd ever owned—they both sucked in sharp breaths. He brushed his thumb against her nipple, which had pebbled under his ministrations, and Flora arched into his touch with a moan.

"Please," she whispered, the only sound possible because his lips had moved to her jaw, her throat.

"Aye, lass." His whiskers scraped the sensitive skin at the base of her throat, but he soothed with more kisses. Then he was bending over her and—

Fudgesicles!

His mouth closed around her other nipple, *through* the linen, and Flora's hips rose off the bed of their own accord.

While his teeth scraped against her sensitive spots—the now-wet material felt both cold *and* hot, somehow—his other hand moved lower. His wide hand spread across her belly, pressing her into the mattress, then lower still, until she was near breathless with anticipation and need.

The heel of his hand settled atop her mound, and her knees fell open. He began to gently rub circles against the little spot hidden among her curls which she'd found on her own to be so responsive...and 'twas *exactly what she needed.*

"Payton!" she gasped again, movements frantic as she yanked on the hem of her chemise, trying to pull it up her legs while also focusing on what his tongue was doing to the second nipple now...

He made a little noise, a hum, which Flora *swore* she felt in her core. 'Twas as if her nipples were directly connected to her—

Oh.

She ceased thinking when the cooler air of the room brushed against her wet core, and his groan sounded almost like one of surrender. His hand moved down atop her curls, his fingers delving into her wetness, stroking, stroking…

"*Aye*," she breathed, eyes tightly shut as she chased the feeling ever higher.

"That's it, lass," he murmured, as he ceased his ministrations to her nipple and straightened. "That's a good lass."

She opened her eyes and met his gaze—his intense, almost *proud* gaze. He held it as he slowly lowered his head.

"What are ye—"

"That's my good lass," he repeated, and her eyes opened wide when he settled himself between her legs.

She pushed herself up on her elbows, trying to see what Payton was doing down there, but he wasn't looking at her any face longer.

Instead, his attention was focused on her core, and Flora caught her breath when she realized what he was about to do.

"Ye dinnae have to—" she began.

That's when he blew softly, and the cooler air hit her heat moments before his tongue did.

Flora fell back against the pillows with a moan.

His tongue's movements were small at first, almost as if he was getting to know her, learning her responses. For her part, Flora couldn't focus on the individual sensations, as everything built together into one overwhelming cataclysm.

When he slipped a finger inside her, she gasped, realizing 'twas just what she'd needed. "More," she groaned, taking her weight on her heels and pushing her hips toward his face. "More…"

She *felt* him smile against her, which should have been impossible, but he obliged her, easing another finger inside. His calluses, his thickness…'twas *everything*.

And still his tongue caressed her.

KILTY PLEA

His gentle thrusts were slow at first, and Flora's hips began moving in tempo as the pressure within her built higher and higher.

And then Payton's mouth closed around the little pearl of her pleasure, hidden in her curls.

Flora exploded.

'Twas no other word for it; she exploded, right then and there in that bed, gasping wordlessly as she came apart.

Her inner muscles squeezed him, milking his fingers, again and again, as he hummed against her clitoris. 'Twas too much, and Flora found her fingers digging into his hair, although she wasn't certain if 'twas to keep him there or thrust him away.

Payton understood better than she, thank goodness.

As the intensity began to abate, he gently pulled his fingers from her, and moved his mouth back to her folds, swiping his tongue through them a few more times for what she supposed was good measure.

Now, *now*, she could feel each little movement, each *heartbeat*, and 'twas nearly overwhelming.

"Payton," she whimpered, tugging at him, needing him.

He understood, bless him.

"Aye, lass." He shifted up beside her again. "That's my good lass."

When he gathered her in his arms, she went, still half in shock. Her body hummed with what he'd just done, and although she'd orgasmed before—thanks to her fingers and active imagination—she never imagined a man would do something like that.

"Come here," he murmured, shifting her so her head rested on his shoulder and her thigh was thrown over his. This allowed her to focus on the dull throbbing in her core, with her chemise still gathered around her hips.

What had *that* been about?

In her previous experiences with men—when she'd arrived

at the Abbey—Flora had learned that they were simple creatures, caring only about their pleasure. Oh, she'd known that sex *could* be enjoyable for a woman, but she'd seen no evidence that men worried about that pleasure.

Payton had shown her unimaginable pleasure, and had done it without expectation of reciprocation. Wait, actually…

She pushed herself up to see him staring at the bed's canopy, his free hand stacked behind his head. When she glanced down his body, 'twas to see him still wearing his kilt, and aye, 'twas tented in the front.

Her hand rested atop his chest, her fingers spread, so she could feel the strong beat of his heart. 'Twould be simple enough to move her hand lower, to caress that erection. To slip her hand beneath his kilt and stroke his cock. To put it in her mouth.

She *wanted* to.

"Payton?"

"Go to sleep, Flora," he said quietly, lowly. Without looking at her.

"But…" She moved her hand down his chest, and in the blink of an eye, he'd captured that hand, pressing it against his stomach.

Then he turned to her and pressed a kiss against her forehead. "Ye dinnae need to do aught ye dinnae want—I mean, do aught for me. Go to sleep, Flora."

She wasn't certain what he was trying to tell her. She *wanted* to do this, to bring him the same pleasure he'd brought her.

But her eyelids *were* heavy, and she felt so *drained* after that explosion of pleasure.

And he was holding her again.

"Go to sleep, lass," he commanded once more.

So, she obeyed.

CHAPTER 8

THE RIDE back to MacIntyre Castle—Payton couldn't call it *home*, not when he'd felt such surprising contentment at the tower house—wasn't silent, but it didn't feel as comfortable as yesterday's journey had been.

Tonight was Hogmanay, and the days would start getting longer. This should be a time of celebration, but he didn't feel it.

His moods were tuned to the woman in his lap, and Flora seemed...*sad*. Withdrawn. A few times, he thought he felt her gaze on his face, but when he glanced down, she was staring over his shoulder, gaze thoughtful.

He wanted to ask what she was thinking of, but also... didn't. Half afraid he wouldn't like the answer.

What would happen, in a few short days, when he had to return to the King's side? Flora could be happy in the tower house—she'd said that. It would be a good home for Lenny, a good place to raise a lad. And bairns—

What? Nay!

He wasn't sure where that thought had come from, and Flora hadn't...

He sighed, ruffling her hair in the process.

Since he'd known her, she'd made it clear all she wanted was to find her brother. She didn't want Payton. She hadn't even understood why he'd lied to his family about her. Last night he'd wanted her *so badly*...but he didn't take what she'd offered.

Because he'd known, ultimately, that she hadn't wanted that.

Not really.

She didn't want *him*.

She'd been offering out of obligation; the same way she'd offered herself to him—for his *use*—the first night of their journey together.

Payton *knew* he looked like a monster from a child's tale. And she'd made it clear from the beginning she was trading her favors—offering her body, going down on her knees—in trade for helping her find her brother. Last night, in fact, she'd only reached for him out of obligation.

But Christ Almighty, he could still taste her.

Feeling her come apart like that, catching her desire on his tongue...Payton didn't think he'd ever be the same.

When he was back at court, surrounded by fancy ladies who sniffed haughtily when he glared at them, he'd remember that taste. He'd pull out his cock and stroke himself, remembering the way she'd called his name and come apart on his face.

Just the memory of the way her exquisitely tight passage had squeezed his fingers kept him hard for the last few miles.

His brother Daniel met them in the courtyard. "Payton! *There* ye are!"

Payton refused to feel guilty about escaping this chaos for a bit. "Da kenned where I was off to. Is aught amiss?"

"Nay." Daniel planted his hands on his hips—his cassock covered by a simple cloak—and glared. "But *I* didnae ken where ye were when yer visitor arrived, asking for ye. Since when are ye friends with holy men?"

Smiling, Payton swung Flora down from the saddle and dropped a kiss on her forehead. "Get out of the cold, lass. I'll deal with my brother."

Chagrined, Daniel offered an abbreviated bow. "Lady Flora, apologies."

She offered his brother a small smile, sent a look toward Payton he couldn't identify, then nodded and hurried toward the main doors.

Payton watched her go, appreciating the swish of her skirts around her rear end—he couldn't help remembering how it had felt to cup that arse—and then sighed and turned back to his brother.

"Now, what were ye saying? Ye're the only holy man I dinnae mind spending time with. The rest of them are judgmental bores." Seeing his brother about to argue, Payton hurried to ask, "Ye're certain he was looking for me?"

"The *MacIntyre Hunter*, he said." Daniel seemed harried, running his hand over his tonsured head. "I've been running ragged up here, otherwise I would've gone with him to look for ye. I sent him to the village."

Payton snorted. "If he found the inn—and the whores—he might no' be back up here 'til midnight."

Since the sun was setting and the torches being lit, amid the bustle around them, 'twas no' an exaggeration. But Daniel's mouth curved into an irritated frown. "Shame, brother, he's an *Abbot*. He wouldn't indulge in pleasures of the flesh like that. Here I am, busting my arse to shepherd souls into Heaven, and *ye* get called on by such a great holy man."

"Well, brother, ye're arse is looking un-busted to me, so 'tis certain I am ye'll get the attention of *all* the holy men soon," Payton said with a grin.

Daniel frowned at him, as if trying to work out the insult,

and chuckling, Payton held out his hand. "We've been visiting the tower house. 'Tis been well cared for—ye have my thanks."

His older brother hesitated, then clasped Payton's forearm. "Ye had a pleasant trip? The house is in good condition, but so small."

Shrugging, Payton knew that mattered naught. "We liked it."

Daniel seemed to light up. "So ye're taking it over from me? I remember ye saying Hunters retire when they marry—are ye hanging up yer sword and *finally* relieving me of the duty of taking care of that place?"

Payton was suddenly glad Flora hadn't heard what his brother had said about retiring. Not when even *he* was certain what the future would bring. So, he forced an easy smile.

"Aye, I'll find a way." And he would. "'Tis unfair to ask ye to continue to live there, when yer dream is here, caring for the MacIntyres."

Daniel pumped Payton's hand enthusiastically. "Thank ye!" Still grinning, he pulled Payton into a hug. "Happy Hogmanay to ye!"

'Twas just the start.

The next hours—as the sun set and the moon rose and the revelry began—were just as chaotic and loud as the Yule had been. Payton didn't have a chance to speak to Flora alone—not that he was certain what he would say.

Instead, the pair of them joined in the celebration. He was delighted to discover that, after two ales, Flora was an enthusiastic dancer.

Well, whirler.

Well, spinner-about-in-circles-while-laughing, at least.

He supposed there hadn't been much opportunity for dancing in her life, but the *joy* in her expression made Payton…

Well, it made him want to swear that she'd always have that.

Somehow, he'd make it the truth.

So, smiling along with her, he took her hands in his and

spun them both until they were so dizzy they collapsed, chuckling, onto one of the benches beside the feast.

He *knew* this change in her—she'd been so quiet and sad earlier—was due mainly to the ale...but Payton had to admit *he* was feeling mellower and more hopeful about the future too.

Sighing, he threw his arm around her shoulder and tucked her up against his side, burying his nose in her hair and trying to hold on to this feeling.

"Midnight!" someone called. "First footing!"

"First footing!" the cry went up, and Payton would've joined in, had he not been so content exactly where he was.

Plastered against his chest, Flora hummed. "First f-footing?" he glanced down at her to see her yawn and smiled in response.

"Surely ye must've celebrated it? If the first person over the threshold after midnight—first night of the year—is a dark-haired man, the household will have good luck and prosperity."

She rolled her eyes and struggled upright, the back of her hand pressed against her mouth, ready to stifle another yawn. "Aye, of course. But this place is a *castle*, Payton. Surely 'tis all staged?"

"Staged?"

"Fishsticks! Ye ken what I mean! For certes, yer mother arranged for a suitable dark-haired man to be standing outside as midnight passed, and he'll knock—"

As if on cue, a knocking rang from the doors down to the armory, and a cheer rose from the gathered MacIntyres.

Flora shot him a wry look as if to say "See?"

Chuckling, Payton heaved himself up off the bench, so he could see over the shoulders of his clansmen who were also clamoring for sight of the first footer.

But the dark-haired man who stepped through...

Unconsciously, Payton lurched forward.

The Abbot.

CAROLINE LEE

What had Daniel said? A holy man—an *Abbot*!—had been looking for Payton.

Fook fook shite fook.

Payton glanced over his shoulder, but Flora's eyes were closed and she was smiling slightly as she slouched on the bench. She hadn't seen the bastard yet.

Unfortunately, when Payton turned back to the crowd, the Abbot was pushing his way toward his corner. Payton took a few steps forward, to meet him, but it did no good; the man's gaze flicked to Flora once before he met Payton's eyes, his grin wide.

"Sir Hunter, 'tis ye, aye! Hard to tell without yer helm!" the man cried, slapping Payton on the shoulder in greeting. "Of course, now I see yer face, I can understand why ye wear it! But it matters no', for the Lord works in mysterious ways, eh?"

Payton fought to keep his expression calm, but his hand still curled into a fist atop his belt, where his sword hilt would've been, had he been any place other than his family's home.

The last place he expected danger.

The Abbot was cheerful and effusive—mayhap the man *had* spent the last hours drinking ale with the whores down at the inn—and now stepped back to study Payton with a proud smile.

"I'm happy to see ye so settled and happy, my son. Married life is treating ye well, eh? I've often said a man is happiest when he's getting his wick wet on a regular basis—at least, that's how I like to live my life." He winked hugely and leaned in to nudge Payton's shoulder again, seeming not to notice the good cheer wasn't reciprocated. "She's a good one, eh? As soon as I saw our Flora, I kenned I needed to save her as a reward for someone special."

St. Bart's blessed tongue! 'Twas difficult to resist the urge to glance back at her, to see if a) she'd noticed the bastard, and b) had heard what he'd said.

A reward.

He'd been *saving* Flora as a reward.

Payton's other hand slowly curled into a fist as well, and he had to fight the urge to throttle the man.

Easy lad. Ignore the ale, making ye do things ye would no' normally.

Oh, nay, he was fairly certain he would *normally* want to strangle the Abbot for what he'd heard of the bastard from Flora.

Aye, but ye're a Hunter. 'Tis yer duty to see men like this punished by the law. Unless he attacks ye, ye must remain calm. Remain calm, then drag his arse to the King for judgment.

But...as much as he hated it, Payton had to admit the Abbot was *allowed* to run his abbey as he wished. The people who joined him were there of their own free will, even if they'd decided later—like Flora—they didn't want to be there.

Och, aye? How'd Flora get there in the first place?

Actually...how *had* she arrived there? She'd said she'd fainted after the bandits attacked her home...

"Why are ye here, Abbot?" he growled, his first words to the man.

"Well, I had a meeting with some new men in Oban." The older man shrugged good-naturedly. "And I thought I'd stop by MacIntyre Castle to see how married life was treating my favorite King's Hunter."

Payton shook his head, keeping his voice low. "Ye ken as well as I, Flora and I arenae truly married."

"It hasnae stopped ye from fooking her up, down, and sideways, eh?" The Abbot winked lewdly. "I did ye a favor, and I want ye to remember that."

Christ, Payton could barely think over the pounding of the blood in his temples. "*What?*" he snarled.

"A favor." Grinning, the Abbot winked again. "An easy way

to wet yer wick, as I said, and she's a fine one. I did ye a favor, and I'll need one soon enough."

A *favor*? "I killed yer bandits!" Payton blurted incredulously. "As ordered by the King himself."

"Aye, a man with the King's ear is a powerful friend." The Abbot winked yet again, but this time 'twas not vulgar. More... cheerful. "There might be more little tasks I could use a friend for, and *ye* owe me a debt now."

What had Flora told him, all those weeks ago when he'd found her waiting for him on the roadside?

That's why we were there—to be useful to him. To be given away...gifted to his friends or used to pay debts.

In order to stop his fist from slamming into the holy man's face, Payton whirled, searching out Flora.

She wasn't on the bench, and his frantic gaze didn't see her.

Stalking away from the Abbot without a word, he reached his brother. "Daniel," he demanded, latching onto his brother's arm. "The Abbot of the Abbey of the People is over there. *Do no'* let him leave, aye?"

He waited until Daniel nodded in excitement and began to push his way through the crowd toward the Abbot, and then Payton turned for the stairs, praying he'd guessed correctly.

When he pushed open the door to his chambers, he blew out a sigh of relief.

Aye, there she was, standing with her back to him, staring into the fire. Her arms were wrapped around her middle, and her shoulders were slumped. Payton took the time to latch the door, so they wouldn't be interrupted.

"Flora?" he asked quietly.

When she glanced over her shoulder at him, he saw the tear tracks, and his chest suddenly tightened.

"Flora!" Chest tight, he lunged across the room to her. "What is it, lass?"

But when he reached for her, she ducked out of his hold, silent tears still rolling down her cheeks.

Seeing her like this—and unwilling to accept his comfort—damned near broke him. "Flora?" he whispered, reaching out again, and she flinched away.

Nay.

Nay, no' Flora.

Payton was used to flinches, used to people winces and looking away from him...but not from *her*. She hadn't, not once.

And he wasn't certain why that was important, but it *was*.

He stood there, in the center of the room, listening to her sniffles, and feeling useless. Useless and helpless, and not certain he should even be here.

Flora had her arms wrapped around her middle, her shoulders hunched. She stood beside the bed, her back to him.

She'd heard what the Abbot had said, obviously. 'Twas terrible timing, for the man to say such hateful things in her hearing.

"Flora?" he whispered yet again, begging her to speak to him.

She sniffed. "Why—" When her voice cracked, she swallowed and tried again. "Why did ye no' fook me last night, Payton? Why have ye no' yet—" A sob interrupted her.

Suddenly wide-eyed, Payton stared at her back.

What?

That hadn't been what he'd expected her to ask, not at all. Was *that* why she was crying?

She was waiting for an answer, and he wasn't certain he could give her one. Not without baring his soul.

"Because," he finally admitted. "I didnae *want* to fook ye."

With a gasp, Flora whirled around, her hazel glare half-hurt, half-murderous. Payton's lips twitched ruefully, and he shrugged.

"I *want* to make love to ye, lass," he said quietly. "Can ye no' understand the difference?"

Her anger had turned to a wide-eyed look of wonder, and when he asked that, she stared at him for a long moment before finally nodding.

"I—" Flora began, before being cut off by another sob.

Payton held his arms out to her, praying she'd accept his comfort—accept *him*. With another sob, she flew to him, wrapping her arms around his waist and pressing her cheek to his chest.

She cried, but not for as long as he thought she might. Och, aye, she soaked the front of his shirt, and he resisted the urge to tease her, the same he'd teased her about drooling on him. Payton stroked her back, and occasionally pressed kisses to the top of her head, and just willed her to take his strength.

At long last, she sniffed. In a muffled voice, she asked, "*Fine*. Why did ye no' *make love* to me last night?"

Payton snorted. "I wanted to."

"Ye didnae."

"Och, I did, lass. *Trust* me."

She pulled away to frown up at him. "Then why...?"

Why didn't he?

With a sigh, Payton pulled her toward the room's single chair. The bed was closer, and likely more comfortable, but this conversation wasn't the kind he needed to have on the bed. Or anywhere near the bed.

Not if he wanted to get through it without kissing her again.

But he wasn't going to survive without touching her, so when he sat, he pulled her into his lap. Just like atop the horse, only this time she could turn toward him and wrap her arms around his neck.

"Last night, Flora..." he began, then trailed off, because he wasn't certain how to finish that thought. He tried again. "Last night, ye were obligated. I brought ye pleasure, aye?" he asked gently.

St. Bart's left elbow, he *knew* he'd brought her pleasure. If he closed his eyes, he'd still be able to *taste* that pleasure, remember the way she'd felt, squeezing him...

She was staring at his chin. "Nae man has ever cared about my pleasure," she admitted in a whisper.

"I care about naught else, love." Once 'twas said, a weight lifted from Payton's shoulders. He'd admitted how he felt about her, and the castle hadn't come crashing down around his head.

"Then..." Gray-green eyes flicked to his, then away. "Why did ye no'..."

Payton sighed and shifted his hold on her. "Because, love. Last night was about *ye*. Ye didnae have to do aught for me."

"I wanted to," she sniffed.

That sounded like a weak argument to him. She peeked up at him again.

"What about the other nights, Payton?"

Every night since they'd arrived and told his family they were married. Every night since he'd kissed her again.

"Ye...were tired?" he tried.

Flora frowned. "I *wouldnae* have been tired if ye'd been kissing me."

Och, she was likely correct. He sighed again, hating that he had to spell this out.

"Because, Flora, *ye* didnae want it."

She suddenly stiffened, her arms falling away from his neck. "W-what?"

"Ye only offered yer body to me afore because ye needed something from me." Payton scrubbed his hand over his face. "Do ye no' understand? 'Tis the only reason *any* woman would offer herself to me! Whores want money, ladies want influence..."

"And I wanted to find my brother," Flora finished dully. "That's what ye think, aye?"

Payton's arm tightened around her for a moment, before relaxing. He had her in his lap now, aye, but he didn't want to make her uncomfortable. "The abbot offered ye to me, as if ye were some kind of chattel, because he wanted me to be obligated to him. Do ye understand, lass? In my world, fooking is about obligation, and I didnae want that."

She was staring at the fire again, and he could see the tears in her eyes. Finally, she said quietly, "Nay."

Nay?

When she turned back to him, her expression fell into a scowl. "*Nay*. When we're together, Payton—and we *will* be together—we will nae be fooking." Anger charged her tone now, and she pushed away from him. "Last night…"

She shook her head as she stood, and he had to curl his hands into fists to keep from reaching for her, pulling her back when she clearly didn't want to be with him.

But to his surprise, she turned and placed her hands on his shoulders, bending closer. "Last night was the first inkling I had that a man could be aught other than painful."

His heart clenched at the thought of a man touching her with something besides reverence, but she went on.

"Last night, ye taught me I was *worth* caring for. I was *worth* pleasure. I was worth…" She shook her head, then took a deep breath, holding his gaze. "And I ken this."

Instead of continuing, she leaned forward and kissed him.

Not on the lips, but on his brow.

Then, her lips dropped to the bridge of his nose, which had been destroyed years ago. Then she kissed the scar under his left eye. She used her fingertips to turn his head so she could kiss what remained of his ruined ear.

And each touch of her lips…was like a brand.

He could feel her in his skin, in his *soul*. He could feel her breath, taste her heart, close his eyes and still see her brilliant light.

'Twas a benediction.

"Last night, Payton," she whispered, "I wanted to bring ye pleasure. No' because ye brought *me* pleasure. No' because I was obligated…but because yer pleasure would bring me joy."

He was having trouble taking a breath, but he understood what she meant. "'Twas why I did it," he admitted.

"Aye." Her lips curled into a grin, and her eyes, so close, suddenly sparkled. Not with tears, but with something else. "And ye must concede it could be the same for me, aye?"

His response was an immediate shake of his head. "Nay."

"Nay?" She frowned, but teasingly. "Why no'? Why could I no' *want* to bring ye pleasure?"

"Because ye are beautiful, Flora, and I'm…" *A monster.* He shook his head. "I'm no'."

"Oh, suck a duck!" She blew out a breath and straightened, her hands going to her hips as she shook her head. "*Suck a duck,* Payton."

His lips twitched at her language. Even when she was being difficult, he loved this woman!

Flora was scowling for certes as she stared down at him. Finally, she reached for his hands. "I'm no' beautiful," she said, pulling him to his feet. "But ye're the only man who's ever said that to me."

"I find that hard to believe."

"Shut up, Payton, and take yer clothes off."

He blinked. "Why?"

"Because, ye dobber." Flora reached up, clapped her hands on either side of his face, and drew him down to her. "I'm going to show ye how beautiful *ye* are."

CHAPTER 9

UNRESISTING, Payton allowed her to push him down to the mattress. They were both nude now, although he'd offered little noises of protest throughout.

The silly man still didn't understand, did he?

"Flora—" he began, but she straddled him, and he nearly bit his tongue off.

"Last night, ye showed me *my* pleasure was important," she whispered to him, moving up his body until her hands were pressed into the bed on either side of his head. She could feel his cock, already stiff, brushing against her arse. "And I want more."

"Aye, lass." His voice was raspy as he settled his hands on her hips. "Aught ye want, I'll give it to ye."

'Twasnae *I love ye*, but 'twas close enough. Flora grinned.

"Good. I was hoping ye'd say that."

Then she kissed him.

It wasn't a desperate sort of kiss, nor a gentle one. More... teasing. She *teased* his lips with hers, and then with her tongue, wondering if he could taste how much she wanted him.

The ale is making ye bold.

Nay, whatever effects the ale might've caused had dried up when she'd seen the Abbot. Hearing his words, hearing how he'd manipulated Payton, and expected to continue to manipulate him...it had made her want to attack the man; to hurt him for the way he'd hurt her, the way he was trying to hurt Payton.

Then she remembered Payton didn't belong to her, not really. *Ye ken as well as I, Flora and I arenae truly married.* Payton himself had said that.

But she *wanted* to be. Running—and the tears—had seemed natural, and until he'd found her, she hadn't been really certain *why* she was crying. But then he was there, and she knew; she was crying for what she'd lost with *him*.

And now, after hearing his stupid reasoning, his attempts to place his own fears in her mouth...Flora knew she'd have to show him the truth.

So, *this* kiss...'twas all about drawing him out. Showing him how much she loved him.

Her lips trailed over his scar, his brows, his hairline. Really, she'd only bothered making *that* move because it moved her breasts into his face, which turned out to be quite a lot of fun. His tongue found her nipples, and a giggle escaped her lips before she could control it.

His hands had slid around to her rear end, his fingers kneading the flesh there. She knew she'd put on weight since arriving at MacIntyre Castle, but would never be *curvy*.

He didn't seem to mind.

She reversed direction, kissing him down his neck again, biting him gently on his collarbone, then licking the spot to soothe it. His groan was barely audible, coming more from his chest than his throat, and when she peeked up, she saw his eyes were tightly shut, his head thrown back.

Oh, did he think this was torture? She'd show him.

Flora shifted her weight down his body until she straddled his thighs, then straightened. His member—jutting tall and proud—rested against the front of her mound, and she sat back so she could peer at it.

His fingertips dug into her hips, but he still wasn't looking at her. Could he *feel* her gaze? Feel how wet she was for him already?

His cock jumped, and she grinned. Mayhap he could.

After only a heartbeat's hesitation, Flora wrapped her fingers around it, and this time he exhaled his groan.

Twas thick, aye, but she hadn't expected otherwise, because Payton was a big man. What surprised her was the feel of it—hard, aye, but yet…somehow soft. The tip was darker than the rest, and as she dragged her palm over him, she felt a bead of moisture seep from it.

She smiled in delight.

"Christ, Flora," he rasped. "Ye're killing me."

"No' yet."

Her experiences with sex had been violent, angry—not something she'd been allowed to explore. But this man? This man was lying there, allowing her to touch him as much as she wanted.

And she did.

She studied him, she felt him. She suspected she might be teasing him, but she was too delighted by this freedom to worry about that.

His cock felt…right.

Last night, he'd touched her, he'd put his mouth on her. And she wanted to do that, but not right now. Right now, her core was aching, weeping…all over his ballocks.

And she knew what she needed to do.

Still holding him, she shifted forward, lifting her weight onto her knees, grinning wickedly. She waited until he met her eyes, then she sat back again…

Only this time, she pressed his cock against her core, sliding her lips over him, and slicking him with her desire.

His eyes widened on a hiss, and her grin grew.

"Beautiful, Payton," she whispered the reminder, and did it again. And again, until his hands rose to her hips, then brushed up her sides. Caressing her, cherishing her.

His breathing was as unsteady as hers.

Finally, deciding they'd *both* been teased enough, Flora reached for his shoulder, steadying herself. Holding his gaze—and his cock—she sank back down atop it.

'Twas thicker than she expected, but also...*perfect*. She took her time, allowing her body to adjust, while Payton's fingers dug into the skin of her arse, his breathing shallow. He was watching her, aye, but making no move.

He was allowing her the freedom to do as she wanted. *Needed*.

After a moment, she felt...itchy. As if she needed to move. So, she did, rocking forward just slightly, allowing his skin to slide over hers in the most wonderous way. He made no reaction, but the skin around his mouth and eyes tightened, and she knew he was struggling to maintain control.

So, she did it again, this time rocking further before sitting back. Still no response. Again.

Each time, the sensation caused her to catch her breath, her focus on the pressure building between her legs, the pleasure mounting there.

And then, she sank *all* the way down atop him, so that the head of his cock seemed to brush against the deepest depths of her, and she whimpered.

"Flora," he rasped, pulling her toward him. *"Jesu Christo."*

'Twas like some spell had broken, and with that, she began to *move*. She moved, and each time she rocked back against him, they both hissed out a breath, until the rocking—the thrusting, the plunging—was too fast, and she could barely do more than gasp occasionally.

The pleasure built and built, and his hands...oh God, his

hands were everywhere. Cupping, holding, tugging. He played with her nipples, he found her arse. And then he tucked his fingers between them, his thumb finding her little nub, and brushing against it gently.

"Pay—" she gasped, not able to finish the rest of the word, as her body convulsed.

She rocked forward, placing her hands on the mattress above his shoulders, leaning toward him...giving *him* control.

Payton understood. With a growl, he slammed upward, his hips bucking beneath hers, his movements almost frantic. One hand held her hip, and the other continued to torture her with the gentle touches.

Her breasts were close enough for him to put in his mouth, but he didn't.

"Look at me, lass," he rasped.

And as her hair fell down around them, blocking the outside world, she did.

She looked deep into his fascinating brown eyes, and she fell.

"Come for me, Flora. Come *with* me."

That command sent her over the edge.

She gasped his name again as her orgasm burst over her, *stretch stretched stretching* by the sensation of him plunging into her core. Each thrust was a tease, somehow expanding her pleasure beyond what she could've imagined.

"Oh, God, *Flora*," he yelled...and she felt liquid heat spilling into her from below. Still, he continued his thrusts—twice, thrice more—and she finally collapsed back atop him, sheathing him to the hilt in her body.

Oh God, indeed.

That had been...

Flora couldn't find words for it, even if she *could* find breath.

That had been life-alteringly magnificent. There. How about *that*?

She'd collapsed awkwardly over him, and she was fairly certain her hair was in his mouth, but he was breathing as hard as she was. Her cheek was pressed to his shoulder, and as their heartbeats calmed, she felt his member soften and slide from her.

Her lips curled into a grin.

He was hers, now, and she was his.

When she rolled off him, they both made a sort of grunt, and he rolled as well, as if unwilling to lose her. They ended up on their sides, facing one another. Faces inches apart.

"There," she whispered. "Do ye understand?"

His warm gaze flicked between hers for a long moment, as if searching for the truth. Then he said, simply, "I am…beginning to."

"I love ye, Payton." She placed her hand on his cheek. "I love ye, no' because ye saved me, no' because ye found my brother and gave him a place. I love ye because ye're *ye*. Because ye're a good man, a caring man, a man who worries about others, and who wants what's best for those around ye. I love *ye*."

Slowly, she watched his expression change. 'Twas like seeing the sun rise, or a trickling stream turn into a waterfall. Until he was smiling.

"I believe ye," he whispered, and there was something like *wonder* in his voice.

"I love ye," she said again, hoping he understood she was speaking the truth. What they'd just shared, it hadn't been about obligation, or bribery, or *manipulation*, as the Abbot had called it.

This had been beautiful.

This had been… She swallowed and closed her eyes.

What they'd just shared had felt like a *forever*.

"Marry me, Flora."

Her eyes flashed opened again, to see his gaze full of some kind of emotion. But it wasn't doubt. It wasn't questioning.

She began to chew on her lower lip.

"Flora, love? 'Tis customary to say something."

"Are ye certain?" When he opened his mouth, she hurried, "Is it what *ye* want?"

With an incredulous look, Payton pushed himself up on his elbow. "How could ye ask that? Of *course* I want it. My family already believes it, after all. I want..." He blew out a breath, his gaze darting around the room as if looking for inspiration as he sat upright. "I want to live in the tower house with ye—I want to turn it into a home. I want to help ye raise Lenny into a strong young man. I want... Christ."

Flora slowly sat up, pulling the blanket up to her chest, watching the play of emotions across his face, and hardly daring to hope.

"I want *ye*, Flora," he finally said, twisting back to her, snagging one of her hands in his. "How could ye doubt that? After what ye just shared with me? I would be a lucky man to spend the rest of my life with ye—for certes this time, no' the false marriage my family believes."

Her gaze was searching his face. "Ye...really mean that?"

"For the love of—ye really are dense sometimes, love," he announced, leaning forward and scooping her into his arms, pulling her against him as he fell backward. She landed atop his chest, her hands caught between them, her breath whooshing out of her lungs. *"I love ye, Flora."*

And then she wasn't breathing at all, because the words... the magical, wonderful words...

He grinned. "If that knocks ye speechless, 'tis a trick I'll have to remember in the future."

"Love a duck, Payton," she breathed, eyes wide.

"Is that one of those cases where nae one ever means *duck*?"

How could he tease her at a time like this? She swatted at

his chest, then placed both palms against him, reveling in the feel of his strong heartbeat. "Ye mean it? Ye really love me?"

"I love yer strength." He pulled her closer to kiss her nose. "I love yer sense of humor." He kissed her brow. "I love the way ye tease me." He kissed her cheekbone. "And I love how well we fit together. No' just *this* way"—he flexed his hips—"but our lives."

She stared down into his eyes, and he grinned.

"Marry me, Flora."

"Yer position…"

He nodded. "I'll write to Drummond, tell him I'm quitting. I'd go in person, but I dinnae want to leave ye—unless ye, and mayhap Lenny, wanted to go with me?"

The last was said in a hopeful voice, but Flora was already shaking her head, pushing herself up out of his arms to have this argument.

"Ye *cannae* quit, Payton! Being a King's Hunter is *verra* important work!"

"Ye've taught me I want a quiet life, Flora. With ye at the tower house, and only having to see my family on special occasions."

She didn't appreciate his jest.

"Ye keep us all safe! Ye protect us from enemies who'll—who'll *manipulate* and hurt us. I mean, aye, I *do* want to marry ye, Payton, but turning in yer helmet…"

Her stomach soured, thinking of the man downstairs. The man who'd come into Payton's home as an honored first-footer guest. The man who'd ruined her life.

Slowly, Payton sat up, taking her with him. "Normally, I'd be thrilled to hear ye accept my proposal, but it sounds to me as if ye're no' talking hypothetically, are ye, love?"

Frantic now, she shook her head, her gaze darting around the room without really landing on aught, trying to find a way to make Payton understand the way her heart had sped up at the thought of him losing his power. "There are men who—who *prey* on those weaker than themselves."

"Flora, the Abbot cannae hurt ye, I promise. He has no power away from his compound."

Nay. Nay, ye're wrong!

Why couldn't she say the words? Her pulse was pounding in her temples, and she twisted away, trying to breathe. "I just dinnae want someone I love to...to be hurt."

He hummed slightly, and placed his fingertips against her cheek, turning her gaze toward him.

"Tell me, Flora," he commanded. "Make me understand."

Fudge buckets.

She took a deep breath.

'Twas amazing how Payton could go from utterly sated to absolute dread in such a short amount of time.

Making love to Flora had been the most magnificent experience of his life, but now he could *feel*—taste, see—her terror, and the pleasure of the last minutes ebbed away. It had been replaced by a very visceral need to learn what had her so scared...and destroy it.

"Tell me, Flora. Make me understand." *Please.*

"The Abbot..." She was looking at Payton, but he could tell she wasn't really *seeing*. "He's no' a good man. No' a holy man. At all."

Payton snorted. "Aye, I could've guessed. There are charlatans who take advantage of the weak-minded, is that what ye mean? Ye're no' weak, Flora, to have been taken in by his lies. Did he promise ye a better life at the Abbey? Is that why ye went there after the attack on yer home?"

She shuddered, and he hated her fear.

"'Tis aright, love," he murmured, gathering her into his lap and tucking her under his chin. "He has nae power here."

"Ye're wrong," she whispered.

"About what?"

She didn't answer for a long moment, then—so quietly he barely heard it—breathed, "All of it."

Payton's first instinct was to deny it. He'd spent most of his life in the King's service, tracking down and punishing evil men, and thought he understood what he was doing. But what kind of man would he be if he didn't listen to the words—the evidence—of those who had actually lived the experience?

"Tell me," he coaxed again.

When she pushed out of his lap, then entirely off the bed, he felt a little bereft. But she began to pace, pulling her hair over one shoulder and plaiting it, and he realized how uncomfortable she was.

He did his best not to notice how *naked* she also was.

"The Abbot rules his people by giving them hope and beatitudes, telling them to work together and share all property. The people who join him willingly...they do it for the reasons ye said; they need those things in their lives, and he makes them feel good about themselves."

She'd stopped in front of the fire, and was now staring into it, her braid hanging half complete, and her arms wrapped around her middle.

"But no' all of us chose to join him."

Payton swung his legs over the side of the bed. "What do ye mean?"

"After the bandits attacked my family's croft, and killed my father, and knocked my brother senseless..." She shivered and trailed off.

He stood, but wasn't certain if he should take her in his arms. His heart ached for her, but he couldn't help her say the words.

Flora shivered, then suddenly darted away from the fire, reaching for her discarded chemise. In a flurry of movement, she pulled the soft linen over her head, and shivered again as it settled around her. She looked positively adorable, standing in her bare feet, with the chemise hanging over one shoulder...but she seemed so lost that he wanted to hug her.

"Come here," he muttered, holding out the tartan blanket from the bed. "Wrap yerself in this."

She stepped near, and he focused on draping it around her shoulders, like the cloak he'd once given her. The fussing helped distract him from the tear tracks on her cheeks.

Fook. From ecstasy to tears in ten minutes.

Flora didn't step back, but tipped her head to meet his gaze.

"The bandits took me to the Abbey. 'Tis far too remote to have found it accidentally—the members who join must really want to be there. But that also means, 'tis too remote to *leave*."

His hands found her hips. "Ye're saying...ye were a prisoner there?"

She shrugged. "In order for the men who join to have the benefits of community, fraternity, and cosmic oneness—or whatever shite the Abbot preaches—the women have to work their fingers to the bone. The Abbot uses those women to keep the men indebted to him; their service, their cooking, the way they—*we*—took care of them." She swallowed, her gaze dropping to his chin. "And sometimes, he offered the women to the men as bribes, or gifts. To keep them happy."

"Or to manipulate them," Payton growled, understanding. "Did this happen to ye?"

She shook her head. "The youngest women slept in the unmarried women's dormitory. We were told we were special, honored...but really, he married us off to the men who'd done him favors, or whose favors he wanted to assure."

Fook. "Like me."

Her breath eased from between her lips, and she nodded. "Like ye."

Well, he'd be damned afore he allowed the Abbot any control over him! Flora hadn't belonged to the man to give away in the first place!

One thing didn't make sense. "The Abbey *is* remote. How did the bandits find ye?"

Flora shook her head, sadness creeping into her features. "Ye dinnae understand. The bandits didn't attack my home and kill my father randomly. They were there for *me*."

Understanding dawned, and Payton's eyes widened. "*St. Bart's earlobe!* They took ye to the Abbey on purpose? Because ye were a young woman? For duck's sake, did they do it on *his* orders?"

Rage was coursing through his veins now, which made her little smile seem odd.

"Ye never *mean* 'duck.' But aye, the Abbot was working with them. Or rather, they worked for the Abbot. In the time I was with him, that same band brought in two other young women, and I have to assume they did it the same way."

"*Fooooooook*," Payton groaned, stumbling away from her and scrubbing his hand over his face. "There's a group of rampaging bandits wandering about the Highlands, attacking vulnerable crofts and stealing lasses, and they're doing it under *his* orders?"

Flora pulled the tartan tighter around her. "Ye killed them, remember?"

"Why?" Suddenly, he dropped his hand and pierced her with a hard gaze. "The Abbot was the one to send to the Hunters and request help vanquishing the bandits. *Why* would he do that, if he was working with them?"

She shrugged. "I dinnae ken."

A calm sense of certainty filled him as he reached for his sword. "Then let us go find out."

"But put on yer plaid first. Else ye'll put someone's eye out with that thing."

How could she be smiling again already? "The blade's in the scabbard."

Flora grin grew. "I wasnae talking about *that* sword."

He glanced down at himself, realized he was still nude, and rolled his eyes, reaching for his kilt instead.

Ten minutes later—aye, wearing the damned kilt—he was pulling Flora down the stairs to the great hall, the rage still pumping through his body. She'd taken time to put on slippers, but still wore only her chemise and the tartan wrapped snuggly around her.

Most of the Hogmanay revelers had passed out or gone to sleep. There were still a few quietly drinking, and on the dais by the hearth, two men sat, speaking animatedly. 'Twas Daniel...and the Abbot.

"There's always a place for a driven young man such as yerself, Father Daniel," the Abbot was saying, his tone inviting conspiracy. "The Abbey has all sorts of benefits for someone who is willing to help."

He was winking just as Payton stomped up onto the dais. His expression faltered for a moment, but the smile he plastered onto his face a moment later seemed forced. "Sir Hunter! I was just extoling the rewards of Abbey life to yer brother."

"Aye," growled Payton. "I've heard all about those *rewards*."

Since Flora joined them at that moment, the Abbot's gaze darted to her—half dressed, hair in disarray, looking as if she'd just come from his bed—and back to Payton. And his grin grew far more sincere...and knowing.

"And I can see ye've been enjoying the benefits of those rewards right now. Is she as wild in bed as I thought she'd be?" he asked with a smirk.

It took everything in Payton's power not to slam a fist into

CAROLINE LEE

the bastard's face. Flora had put her hand on his arm, reminding him they needed answers.

"Why are ye here, Abbot?" she asked in a clear voice.

The man glanced at her again, then made a flicking motion with his fingers and turned his attention back to Payton. "I had a meeting with a group of men in Oban. I was hoping, if ye found the *rewards* pleasant enough, Sir Hunter, ye might consider returning with me to the Abbey, and leading those men."

"These men. They're the kind who are willing to follow orders that might no' be exactly…legal?"

The Abbot shrugged, a knowing glint in his eye and a smug grin on his lips.

Payton wanted to break him.

The arsehole was not only recruiting more bandits, but assumed Payton would be so grateful for being given Flora, he'd do aught the Abbot requested.

Ye are grateful for Flora.

Och, aye, he was, but not enough to help this bastard with aught.

Calmer now, he stepped around the table until he was within reach of the Abbot.

"Let me ask ye a question," he said in a deceptively mild tone. "If ye are hiring more bandits to do yer bidding—travel about the Highlands, finding lonely and unsuspecting lasses, then murdering their families and bringing the women to ye—why'd ye ask the Hunters to help rid ye of the last band who worked for ye?"

The Abbot smirked and leaned back, completely at ease. Payton must've convinced him he was only curious, and that Flora's favors were worth compromising his honor.

"That scum thought they kenned better than I did. Their *leader*"—the Abbot flicked his fingers dismissively—"demanded another wife, since he'd used up his first one so quickly. He said he'd go to the King himself. I had to have them removed." He grinned. "And now I have ye instead."

"Do ye?" Payton growled, the moment before his fingers wrapped around the man's throat.

He had the satisfaction of seeing genuine fear race across the Abbot's expression before Payton's fist smashed into the man's nose. When the bastard slumped in his hold, Payton dropped the unconscious body across the table.

"Payton!" Flora cried, throwing herself into his arms. "That puir woman!"

"Aye, lass," he agreed, turning to find his brother standing with his palms on the table, peering at the man he'd only just been chatting with, incredulity on his face. "Daniel?"

"Was that man as evil as he sounded?"

"Eviler," Payton assured his brother, with conviction. "I'll be taking him to the King to face justice. His Majesty needs to ken no' just of the Abbey, but the bastards the Abbot has been hiring to do his dirty work. This is bigger than me—someone will have to be sent to the Abbey to divide the resources and ensure the lasses are compensated, and that nae one will take over the place."

Thank duck, Flora was nodding. "And ye'll need me to go along with ye, aye? Because ye cannae stand to be parted from me?"

Payton grinned. "That too. And because I'll need yer testimony, if ye're strong enough to share it, lass."

"Aye." She looked grim but nodded. "If it'll help the others, I will. No' all of them are lucky enough to be given to a man who'll help them find and raise their brothers."

St. Bart's arse crack, he loved this woman!

"Thank ye, Flora," he rasped, gathering her in his arms. "Thank ye for allowing me to save ye."

Her lips twitched. "Thank *ye* for loving me, Payton."

Daniel cleared his throat. "Should I go find someplace to lock up this man?"

"I was thinking the storeroom down in the kitchens," Payton confessed, nudging the Abbot with his toe. "When we head to court, I'm taking a contingent of MacIntyre warriors, and I dinnae care what Da or Rupert have to say."

His brother was nodding. "They'll no' stand in yer way. I'll take him down there now and find someone still sober enough to stand guard."

"Aye, but no' yet," Payton hurried to say. "I have an important task for ye first."

Daniel lifted a brow. "More important than securing this bastard?"

Payton looked down at the woman in his arms. "I love ye, Flora, and want to spend the rest of my life with ye."

"I love ye, Payton," she whispered fiercely. "I'm the luckiest woman alive, to have found ye. I cannae wait to start on my forever with ye."

Smiling, Payton looked at his brother. "We need ye to marry us. Here. Now. For real this time."

Laughing at his brother's incredulous look, Payton claimed Flora as his own.

CHAPTER 10

"To yer wife, Payton!" Craig laughed as he punched Payton's shoulder with his free hand, and guzzled ale with his other.

Unfortunately, since Craig Oliphant was the size, shape, and intelligence of an ox, when he punched a shoulder, it stayed punched.

"Ow!" Good-naturedly, Payton rubbed the bruised area. "Ye can admire her without hurting me, eh?"

The other man snorted. "Ye hang up yer helmet and retire, and within a fortnight ye've gone weak? Marriage does that to a man, eh?"

"Weak? My Flora doesnae think me weak!"

Craig shrugged. "Well, she's a wee sprite of a lass, eh? She likely prefers a weak man like ye, who'll no' crush her."

"I'm no' weak!" Scowling, Payton reached for his own ale.

His friend was wearing an expression of sympathy. "That's aright, Pay. I'll no' tell her of her ill-will. She likely doesnae even realize a man's cock can fill her—"

"My cock can fill her—och, why am I having this argument?"

"Because ye're ashamed of yer weak, wee cock," Craig explained seriously. "'Tis aright, I understand. No' all men can be as well-endowed as I—"

With a growl, Payton launched his own punch at his friend, who dodged, laughing.

Instead of blocking the subsequent attacks, Craig merely leaned forward and wrapped his arms around Payton, pinning his arms at his side.

Payton gave up struggling. "Get off me, ye ox. Did nae one tell ye ye're supposed to bathe afore accepting an invitation to a celebration?"

"I bathed! Twice!" Craig was grinning when he released Payton and straightened. "I couldnae risk losing the chance to impress yer family. Do ye have any unmarried sisters?"

"Stay away from my sisters." Payton scowled, but there was no heat in it. In truth, he was *happy*.

Happy Craig was here, celebrating Payton's new life.

Happy the Abbot was safely in the gaol on the King's orders, awaiting execution.

Happy the Abbey was being disbanded, and all the people taken care of.

He was even happy his family was here at the tower house tonight, helping Payton and Flora start their new lives together.

And Flora...

Ah, Flora.

He was *beyond* happy to have her as his forever.

Daniel had married them a month ago, on Hogmanay. He'd done it quietly and without questions, and Payton appreciated that he hadn't had to explain to his family why he and Flora weren't actually married in the first place. His brother was settling into his new role as the priest of MacIntyre Castle, and was grateful.

Flora had come with Payton—and a dozen MacIntyre

warriors—to deliver the bound Abbot to Drummond. She'd stood brave and strong at Payton's side as she'd given her story first to the commander of the Hunters, then to the King himself. After, she'd cried in Payton's arms, but it had been worth it; the Abbot would be punished, and her father avenged.

Then, Payton had held her in his lap on the return journey, marveling at this woman who loved him despite his flaws.

It had been Mam's idea to celebrate the start of his new life with a feast. Flora had agreed but had refused help in planning it. She was becoming confident in her ability to run a small keep like the tower house, and Payton loved to watch her grow.

"Ye love her, do ye no'?"

Craig's rumble drew Payton's attention from where his eyes had been following his wife. "Aye, of course I love her. I married her, did I no'?"

"Plenty of people marry for reasons other than love. But I'm remembering a conversation ye and I had at Barclay's wedding last summer. Ye said ye'd no' marry one of the spoiled ladies at court."

Payton remembered that. He sat back in the large chair he'd had commissioned for the hall in the tower house. "I did."

"And I'm thinking ye were right." Craig nodded toward where Flora was chatting with her new mother-in-law, seeming at ease in her own home. "Yer new wife is aught but spoiled."

"She's a simple lass." Payton took a sip of the ale, smiling. "One who is happy here with me."

"Ye cannae ask for aught more," his friend said, then started. "Och, Lenny! I didnae see ye there."

Payton twisted to see Flora's brother standing solemnly at his side. "Ye snuck up on us, lad. Are ye enjoying yerself?"

Lenny's nod was solemn, and Payton had to smile. "Yer sister created the menu, and she told me she even made the bread." A pause, just in case the lad had any response. "She said she used to enjoy making bread in yer father's home."

The lad just studied him.

Payton was becoming used to the fact Lenny only spoke to Flora. Luckily, he answered direct questions—as long as they could be answered with a nod—and he made his wishes known.

"I ken ye must miss yer da," Payton offered softly, "but Flora and I made certain he's been avenged. And ye ken ye have a place here with us. I'll teach ye all ye need to ken to grow to be a good man, a strong man."

Lenny's gaze flickered across Payton's ruined visage. And for the first time, the man realized this lad hadn't once flinched away from his scars.

Just like his sister.

Finally, Lenny took a deep breath and offered his hand. "I'm pleased ye married her, Payton. Thank ye for making her happy."

Payton gaped.

He gaped, then—after the pause became awkward—reached out to clasp the lad's forearm and pull him forward into a hug. He wrapped his arm around this young brother-in-law of his and muttered against his hair, "My pleasure, lad."

"Hello, my darling Pay-Pay!" When Mam bustled up, Flora in tow, Payton released Lenny and they separated. "What a delightful home ye've built! I'm so pleased for ye, my schmoopy-kins. Flora is turning out to be quite the perfect wife for ye!"

Behind her back, Flora rolled her eyes, and Payton didn't bother hiding his grin.

"Aye, Mam, she is," he announced, standing and reaching out a hand to Flora. When she took it, he pulled her up against his side. "I'm a lucky man."

"Ye are!" His mother patted his arm. "I always kenned my

sugarplum would settle down and give me more grandbairns where I can see them. I just wished ye lived closer, my little sweetmeat, so I could visit ye all the time."

Payton very deliberately did *not* look at Flora, but could feel her barely controlled laughter, even so.

"Yes," he deadpanned to his mother. "That is a shame."

Flora turned and buried her face in his shoulder, hiding her laughter.

"Och, look at that, Lady MacIntyre," Craig announced. "Ye've overwhelmed her with yer praise. What do ye say ye let me distract ye for a bit?"

"What?" Mam seemed confused. "Why?"

Craig nudged Lenny. "So these two can go be alone somewhere, eh? Do ye dance, milady?"

The lad seemed to pick up on the hint and bowed solemnly to Payton's mother. Mam seemed confused when she gave her hand, then peered back over her shoulder when Craig and Lenny tugged her away.

Flora burst into laughter.

"Dingleberries! I dinnae think I could listen to aught more of her *helpful suggestions*. At least Anna is sweet enough to sound impressed when I give her a tour. Yer mother is judging *everything*."

"Thank ye for putting up with her." Payton dropped a kiss to her forehead as he wrapped his arms around her. "I'm glad 'tis a full day's journey, and they'll all be leaving tomorrow."

"I am too," she admitted with a sigh. "I miss our quiet. And our privacy."

Payton hummed thoughtfully. "Ye ken…Craig *is* distracting her. I owe him. We could…retire early."

"Really? From our own celebration?"

He shrugged. "Who cares?" Just the thought of being alone with her was stirring his blood, and now he flexed his hips forward, so she could feel his stiffening cock. "They'll go on celebrating, and we can…be alone."

Flora's grin bloomed. "I think that's a fine idea, husband."

"Lass," he groaned as Flora threw her leg over his thighs and lifted her weight to hover over him, "how'd I get this lucky?"

"Luck has naught to do with it, Payton MacIntyre," she breathed, reaching between her legs to grasp his swollen member. "I love ye for yer heart and yer mind and yer soul."

His fingers dug into her thighs, urging her lower. "Is that all?" His grin was positively wicked.

"Well…" Flora gave his shaft a few teasing strokes. "Also for yer body."

"Christ, woman, I love ye."

Feeling powerful, she slowly lowered herself atop his cock. Both of them sucked in a breath when he was fully sheathed, and Flora gave a toss of her hair so she could smile down at him. "Ready, husband?"

Without waiting for his approval, she began to rock, sliding her wet core along his cock. 'Twas a gentle sort of lovely, one of her favorite things.

She loved how the *need* could build in her slowly, with each teasing brush of the tip of his cock against that secret spot deep inside her.

She loved the way Payton's eyes closed and his head dropped back, the lines around his mouth the only indication of his fight for control.

And she loved how he *allowed* her this control, this chance to build her pleasure, despite it being torture for him.

One of his hands found her breast, urging her forward until he could capture it with his mouth. The sensation of his tongue on her nipple, as she slid along his cock, catapulted her into the stars.

"Payton!" she gasped.

And he understood. 'Twas time for *him* to take control.

With a growl, he wrapped his large hands around her waist and rolled, taking her with him, until she was beneath him on the mattress. He planted his knees and his palms, and Flora spread her knees in anticipation.

His thrusts were strong, fast. Each one seemed to freeze that pleasure she'd built moments ago, holding it in place, teasing her for an impossibly long time. She wanted to explode, aye, but she also wanted to stay in this state forever; this *almost almost almost* moment that made her heart race and her breathing shallow.

"Flora," he gasped, his warm brown eyes boring into hers. "*Now.*"

Her lips curled upward and she wrapped her legs around his arse, as he reached between them.

When his thumb brushed against the pearl of her pleasure, Flora's orgasm burst over her. "Payton!" she cried, arching her back into his thrusts. At the same time, he growled, freezing, as a flood of liquid heat poured into her.

Yes.

Panting, he collapsed atop her as her inner muscles squeezed at him, milking every last sensation from their pleasure. Her hips still rocked, and he began to chuckle.

Payton wrapped his arms around her and rolled them both to their sides so they were facing one another, breathing hard. Staring into her eyes, he used one callused fingertip to brush the hair from her face.

"I love ye, wife."

"Mmm," she agreed with a smug smile, trying to get her breathing under control. "Because I let ye fook me."

He snorted. "Fooking? Nay, 'twas making love, ye daft woman."

Smiling, she allowed her hand to slide up his flank. This husband of hers was so strong, so capable...and so very loving. He'd hung up his helmet, retiring as one of the King's Hunters, but she knew he would still keep the peace here in their little corner of Scotland. He was helping her raise Lenny to be a good man, and maybe—*maybe*—there'd be bairns at some point down the road. Bairns to raise to be good people, as well.

Really, was it any reason she was grinning?

"Stop that, lass," he ordered, capturing her hand in his.

"Why?"

He wasn't fooled by her innocent tone. "*Because*. If ye keep that up, I'll have to take ye again, no choice, ye understand. And a man only has so much seed he can spare. Ye've taken it from me once already—nay, twice if ye count this morning. My puir cock can only handle so much."

"Ahh," she agreed, nodding sagely, even as she nudged him over to his back. "I understand. It must be expected for man of yer age and position to weaken."

"*Weaken?*"

Ignoring his indignant tone, she continued her soft strokes, each time coming closer to the patch of hair between his legs. From the corner of her eyes, she watched his cock twitch, and smiled wider.

"Aye, Payton. Now that ye're married, 'tis up to me to ensure ye maintain yer strength and stamina." With that, her fingers brushed along his soft cock, stroking all the way to his ballocks.

He started. "How—" he began, his voice choked.

Grinning wickedly, Flora positioned herself over him on her knees. She wrapped her hand around his member, which was now stiffening again, and shot him a glance.

"Why, with kisses."

When she lowered her lips to his tip, she tasted their love. While once the thought of this had been horrifying, something she'd only do in order to save Lenny, now...

"Flora."

His tone stopped her, and she lifted her head to see Payton staring at her, his expression inscrutable.

"Love, ye dinnae have to do this."

She frowned. "Ye put yer mouth on *me*, Payton. I cannae do it to ye?"

"Nay, of course—I just mean, ye dinnae *have* to."

Something like *guilt* shifted in his eyes, and suddenly Flora understood. He was remembering their first night together, when she'd lowered herself to her knees and reached for his cock, thinking to manipulate him into taking her with him to MacIntyre land.

"Payton," she breathed, shifting so she could brush her lips across his jaw, while still holding his cock. "I *love ye*. Even then, I kenned ye were a good man, and I was desperate to stay with ye."

"Desperate," he repeated doubtfully.

"Do ye ken, even then, kneeling afore ye...I was confused by my body's reaction to ye?"

"Ye hadnae seen my face."

She kissed him again and squeezed his cock. "I didnae need to. I already kenned ye were brave and strong and oh-so-gentle." When he snorted, she brushed her lips against his. "Do ye remember rubbing my feet? Nae one had cared about me like that—cared *for* me. I was used to taking care of others, and here was this man I had been given to, who didnae want me, who was *caring* for me." Another squeeze. "I just kenned I had to stay with ye."

His voice was strained when he admitted, "I needed ye too, lass. More than ye'll ken."

She grinned. "Well then, I'd say we ended up exactly where we were meant to be."

When he exhaled, his lips curled. "I do love ye, lass."

"And I love ye, Payton. Now…" She pushed herself up onto her knees again and sent him a naughty wink. "Stop fussing. This will be fun."

As her lips closed around him, he laughed, and 'twas the sweetest sound she'd ever heard.

EPILOGUE

LAUGHING, Craig kicked the ball back toward the cluster of children—both lads and lasses—who were teasing him. "Och, ye think ye can gang up on me? Eight against one?"

"Ye can count that high?" taunted one, kicking the ball to a friend, keeping it out of Craig's reach.

The Hunter growled in mock-warning, spread his arms, and ran at the group. They split apart, squealing in laughter, as he lunged about, grasping with hands the size of their heads.

"Here!" one of them called, lobbing the ball at him. He used his head to bounce it back to the lad, even as he scooped up one lassie.

"A trade!" he bellowed, holding the girl above his head, trying to maintain his good-natured scowl in light of how hard she was laughing and squirming. "Whose is this? I'll trade ye for the ball!"

"That's John's sister!" one boy yelled, laughing. "Ye can keep her!"

The rest mobbed Craig, however, and eventually he lowered the laughing girl to be with her friends. "Me! Me!" another lassie was crying. "Do me next!"

The ball game was forgotten as he lifted each of the children over his head and spun them in a circle, until he was dizzier than they were, and collapsed on the snow-covered ground.

"Get up, get up!" they cried, nudging him with their boots—which some might call *kicking*—and chortling. "Again!"

Craig was large enough that he barely felt their nudges. "Nay, away with ye!" he growled, swiping his arm back and forth, as if to grab them. "Let me die in peace."

One young lassie—was it John's sister?—threw herself across his chest. "I'll protect ye, Sir Hunter! Leave him alone! Can ye dobbers no' see he needs his rest?"

Chuckling, Craig pushed himself upright, sitting cross-legged on the cold ground and holding the lassie in his lap. Now she was patting his chest, and he was torn between being offended that she thought he needed protecting, and touched by it.

Actually...there was a strange aching in his chest in the vicinity of his heart.

This perfect, wee creature, with her wild curls and tiny nose, had enough love in her heart to care about *him*?

"Careful, lassie," he managed past a sudden lump in his throat. "Ye shouldnae be using such nasty language."

"Why no'?" the cherub asked, tipping her head back to meet his eyes boldly. "My brothers do."

Craig shrugged, and admitted she was right. "Well, if they use it, then I suppose ye can too."

"I'm just as good as they are, aye?"

"Aye, princess," he murmured, rolling to his feet and taking her with him. "Ye can do aught yer brothers do."

"Except piss standing up," she explained solemnly.

Craig lifted her under her arms until she was eye-level with him. "Then ye're no' trying hard enough."

The wee one burst into laughter and began squirming. "Put me down, Sir Hunter! I want to practice pissing standing up!"

In fact, turned out *all* the girls wanted to try that, and they ran off, laughing and shouting, as the lads returned to their game of kickball. Craig, still chuckling, brushed snow from his shoulders, not realizing he was being watched.

"Ye are good with them."

The quiet voice startled him; instinctively he flexed his knees and whirled, raising his hands into a defensive gesture. But 'twas just Daniel, Payton's aulder brother. The priest stood with his hands tucked into his warm cassock, smiling at the antics of the children.

"The children enjoyed playing with ye," he explained, his brown gaze flicking to Craig, and away. "Do ye have many of yer own?"

Craig startled again at the thought. "Nay, I—" He'd been about to explain how he'd always been careful to spill across a lass's stomach, but he remembered who he was speaking to. "I'm no' married."

The curl of the priest's lips told him Daniel guessed what he'd been about to say, but the man merely hummed. "Have ye considered it?"

"Marrying? Or becoming a father?"

"Either. Both." Daniel shifted, the snow cracking under his boots. "I believe Mam is still trying to marry off two of my sisters."

A surprised laugh burst from Craig's lips. "Nae offense, Daniel, but I'd rather no' have yer mam as a mother-in-law, no matter how bonny yer sisters are!"

The priest merely shrugged. "I dinnae blame ye, I suppose. But 'tis clear ye have much to offer a wife—"

"Ye're wrong. I used to be a blacksmith, ye ken, afore I vowed my sword to the King. But my smithy back on Oliphant land was taken over by my apprentice, and now I live in hired rooms in Scone. I have naught to offer a wife."

Daniel turned to him, facing him completely, that small, enigmatic grin still curling his lips. "Nay, Craig, I didnae mean ye have much to offer a wife in terms of material goods. I meant *here*."

To Craig's surprise, the priest reached out and pressed his palm against the larger man's chest. Right above his heart.

Daniel nodded once, then withdrew his hand and, without speaking, turned and drifted away.

Craig watched him go, mouth agape.

Much to offer a wife?

He...he had naught. He stared down at his hands. He was big, aye, and strong, but he knew the others joked he was dumb as an ox. He was a simple man.

Not the kind a lass might want to yoke herself to for the rest of her life.

But bairns...

Aye, bairns would be fun to have in his life, and the way to get that would be to marry. But who would want to marry a man like *him*?

Craig shook his head and exhaled, the fog obscuring his gaze for a moment.

Nay, marriage and bairns weren't for him. He'd content himself with playing here for a bit longer—mayhap the lads would let him back into the kickball game—before returning to Scone and his next mission.

And he'd put aside that fierce hope Daniel's words had planted in his heart.

Marriage was not for him.

AUTHOR'S NOTE

ON HISTORICAL ACCURACY

You know, *sometimes* I get docked points because people claim I'm not *entirely* historically accurate. Can you believe that? So, in the interest of full disclosure, and teaching you something, I have to admit something:

All those phrases Flora used, like *suck a duck* and *son of a biscuit*? Those were historically inaccurate.

Well, *actually*.

When we read/write medieval Scottish romance, there are things we expect our characters to say: *nae* instead of *not*, *verra* instead of *very*, *mayhap* instead of *maybe*…that sort of thing.

I once had a big argument with an editor because I wanted my heroine to call her father "Papa," and she insisted that was a French word and I needed to use "Da," because that's what readers expected. And she was right.

But so was I.

Because here's the thing that we all know and understand deep down: despite the fact I've never stated exactly *when* these books take place (see earlier Author's Notes), we know the characters wouldn't have been speaking the English we're speaking now. We add *nae* and *verra* and *mayhap* and *Da* to the

AUTHOR'S NOTE

dialogue to give them a Scottish flair to the English language, but they would've been speaking something totally different.

So the point is:

It actually *is* possible that some medieval lady somewhere *did* yell "Love a duck!" or "Cheese and crackers!" when she became irritated…she just did it in Gaelic.

And *that*, my friends, is how you defend the use of "fragglerock" in a medieval Scottish historical romance.

<serious academic nod>

(Although the auto-correct "no one means *duck*" jokes probably didn't work back then. Unless there's a hidden technology I don't know about.)

Moving on…

In past Author's Notes I've talked about medieval Scottish holiday traditions, most especially Yule and Hogmanay (New Years), but we can do a basic overview here again.

The most commonly recognized is the Yule Log, the large log/tree (often oak or ash) that would be chosen and dragged into the home to be burned in the hearth. In a castle or large estate, that log could be massive (those hearths were huge!). Burning this log symbolized warmth, light, *et cetera* in the middle of the darkest part of the year.

Similarly, there could be a large candle, or many smaller candles, lit to symbolize the return of the light. Remember, the days start getting longer again on December 22, so this is the time of year to celebrate surviving the worst of the winter.

As you can imagine, greenery brought indoors would have similar symbolism, referencing the coming spring, and feasting and gift-giving would accompany all this good-will and cheer.

The ale helped.

As for Hogmanay, the most commonly known tradition is "First Footing", referring to the first person to enter a home after midnight on New Year's Day. As Flora pointed out, it's often staged, to ensure that the dark-haired man is carrying the

AUTHOR'S NOTE

traditional offerings of whisky, bread, and coal (three things important to keep a family going through January!).

In a previous Author's Note, I delved deeper into the idea of the dark-haired man...why should he be dark haired?

The short answer is basically: There were times in Scottish history (coughTheVikingInvasioncough) when a blond-headed stranger showing up at your front door was considered very bad luck indeed.

So, even as a blonde myself, I can totally understand where the tradition of a dark-headed stranger bringing luck got started.

Okay, that's probably a good segue into talking about the medieval church and marriage traditions, and why I turned them on their head in this book.

(Subtle, Caroline, real subtle.)

There's actually a lot of interesting stuff that went on in the medieval church, my favorite of which was that a lot of local priests often had lovers, common-law wives, and even families, which is just adorable. None of that is relevant, I just wanted to share.

(Actually, there's a lot of reasons that the Catholic Church declared priests should be celibate...*but* one of the most practical outcomes meant that they couldn't marry and produce heirs, so there wasn't any confusion about inheritance. Imagine if the local priest *could* marry and begat a legitimate heir; would that son think *he* should inherit the building and the gold chalice and the right to collect alms from the congregation? By declaring priests unable to marry, the Church assured that Church property would *remain* Church property...although there were cases of a village priest begetting an illegitimate son who grew up to take vows and become the next village priest... both of them sworn to the Church.)

Okay but no, seriously that's not relevant to this story Caroline, move on.

AUTHOR'S NOTE

The point is: the Church was this super-important presence in medieval life, offering solace and comfort, the hope of a better life after you're done with this one.

But Scotland was a long way from Rome (or wherever the Pope happened to be hanging out those days—for a while he was in Avignon, France), and rules didn't always get followed exactly.

It might not have been clear, but in my mind, the Abbot in this story wasn't a holy man at all, but merely a man who decided to use humanity's need for leadership and comfort to create his own little commune. "The Abbey of the People" was based heavily on some of the cults that sprang up in America in the '70s, with a charismatic leader and members desperate for something different and meaningful.

Which in itself is a bit ironic, because some of the communes that became popular during that time (the 1970s) were based on the almost-medieval idea of a community of people working together and sharing resources.

The point is: the Abbey in this book isn't an actual religious place, and I hope that was obvious.

Right, okay, moving on to our last point: Medieval marriage traditions.

First of all, marriages happened in a church. With a priest. A *Catholic* one. When the Pope excommunicated King John down in England, and the clergy had to flee, Scotland was still doing hot business as a Catholic country.

So, marriages were performed by a priest.

But there are also traditions which are uniquely Scottish, developed separately from the Catholic Church.

Handfasting is likely the most memorable one; the idea that a couple could "try out" marriage for a year and a day has a romantic endurance. Hell, even my wedding included the pastor symbolically wrapping our hands in his stole.

I will caution you that *if* handfasting was practiced (and it

AUTHOR'S NOTE

was actually much less common than Historical Romance leads us to believe), then it was always to the man's benefit. He was "trying out" the woman to see if she would make a good wife, by which we mean, get pregnant and hopefully present him with a son.

If a year and a day went by and she *hadn't* gotten pregnant (or didn't make good bread, or sucked at sweeping, or however else he judged "good wifeyness" by), then he could end the arrangement and he'd be free to go find another wife, while she'd be labeled as Bad Wife Material.

I made that up, but now I kinda want to form a band by that name.

Anyhow, some of the lesser-known medieval marriage traditions included the Luckenbooth brooch (entwined hearts inscribed with the couple's initials) and the Scottish quaich cup.

The quaich cup isn't solely a wedding tradition, but used in any ceremony bringing two people together; like a peace treaty or a welcoming celebration. It's often shallow, almost like a bowl, with two handles. Each person (or representative) takes a handle, and together you drink (or help one another drink) to symbolize unity, cooperation, and goodwill.

In a wedding, you can drink whatever you'd like out of the quaich cup, but as you can imagine, whisky is often chosen.

It was this tradition that I used when coming up with the "marriage ceremony" at the Abbey. It's so simplistic (drinking offered milk from a bowl) that Payton didn't realize what was happening, but also rooted in the quaich tradition.

The whole *not being married by a priest* thing was a bit problematic, though.

Well, yet again I've managed to blather on for too long about accuracies and inaccuracies in the story, so I hope you've learned something. I'd love to hear from you (email me at Caroline@CarolineLeeRomance.com) either way!

AUTHOR'S NOTE

And as always, please do come hang out in my reader group, or sign up for my newsletter to get free books (actually, if you sign up for the newsletter, you'll receive a book which isn't available for sale anywhere, which is pretty cool!).

Thanks for hanging out with me, and I'm glad you had fun!

Printed in Great Britain
by Amazon